A Season to Love

By K. McCoy

A Season to Love

K. McCoy

Published by be a muse productions, LLC, 2022.

A SEASON TO LOVE

First edition. December 6, 2022.

ISBN: 979-8991737623

Written by K. McCoy.

Table of Contents

Dedication

TO THOSE OF YOU WHO believe in love, this is for you. That generous, all-encompassing, and overwhelming love that brings out the best in whomever receives it. I hope for those of you that are looking and are willing, ready, and able to give that kind of love to another, I hope that you all find it and experience it for the rest of your days.

Happy Holidays!

K. McCoy

Holiday Butterflies

L ove is in the air, and in both Shinee and Taeyang's hearts, as they spend their first holiday together as a couple. Though for Taeyang, he wants to secure their happy ever after this winter and has planned the most harmonious way to do just that.

Will Taeyang's confession on Christmas go off without a hitch, or will he and Shinee end up with the Christmas blues?

Chapter One
A Concert for Lovers

He watched as the sun danced across Shinee's deep chestnut skin. Taeyang almost envied how its touch seemed to electrify her glow. Thinking back on the last three years that the two have spent together, Taeyang found his gaze on her alluring face.

And she still chose me. This is my person, in every way. He thought to himself. *My beautiful butterfly.*

Unable to stop himself, Taeyang tucked away the stray puffy loc that fell over her sleeping face. His smile grew wider as he thought about the secret surprise that he had in mind for later that day.

"Are you that happy just looking at me?" Shinee mumbled.

So distracted by his thoughts, Taeyang didn't notice her waking up. Those thoughts now took a playful turn as he leaned in closer towards her face and brushed their noses together. Shinee's giggles warmed his heart, but her hands as they swatted at Taeyang's bare chest warmed more. Taking her hand into his, Taeyang locked eyes with Shinee before he half seriously asked. "Do we have to go out today?"

Shinee's laughter grew louder as she tugged her hands away from his.

"This trip was all your idea, and you can't change your mind now! Not when my favorite Seoul crooner is about to perform in..." She squinted while looking at the clock on the nightstand behind him. "Five hours! Oh, why did you let me sleep so late?!"

It was now Taeyang's turn to laugh as Shinee stumbled out of bed. He propped his head up with the help of a pillow and watched as she sprinted to the bathroom and talked to herself in between brushing her teeth. Soon, two rainbow colored socks went sailing into the air, along with a satin bonnet cap and Taeyang finally left the warm bed to investigate. He leaned against the bathroom wall and quietly watched Shinee flurry about while getting dressed. Now done with washing up, she flung around articles of clothing, only pausing to press a few pieces against her chest to ponder over as she stared into the mirror. Then just as quickly, Shinee placed the discarded clothes back into her suitcase.

"Why did you let me pack so many things?" She asked in dismay.

Taeyang smirked before answering her. "Could I have been able to stop you, had I tried to?"

The two looked at one another before smiling. Suddenly remembering his plans for the day, Taeyang turned away and began getting dressed as well. He waited patiently for Shinee to go back into the bathroom before he placed his second, and more hopeful gift for her into the breast pocket of his coat.

"Is this okay?"

Taeyang slowly turned back around and took his time admiring Shinee in her deep green sweater dress. It stopped just before her knees and Taeyang found himself chuckling at the red and gold dancing reindeer socks that she wore. Shinee followed his gaze and pouted. "No one will even see my socks once I put on my knee high boots! Besides, it is too cold to go out without these on my toes."

Strolling towards her, Taeyang took her hands into his as he stared into her wide, doe-like eyes. "You are beautiful. I would not change anything about you. My sweet butterfly."

Shinee leaned toward him and kissed him quickly on the cheek, but he still managed to see the faint blush spreading across her warm brown skin from his words.

The venue for this indoor Christmas Jazz concert was larger than Taeyang originally thought it would be, and a quiet storm waged on in his head about whether or not he would be able to follow through on what he had planned. Just as he began to reconsider, Shinee linked one of her hands into his and winked at him, calming him without knowing it. He felt the heat begin to rise to his cheeks again as he stared at her.

"Thank you."

Shinee looked puzzled for a moment before she asked. "Thank you? What did I do to receive thanking for, my sunshine?"

Taeyang's smile grew wider upon hearing the new nickname, and in that moment, the small wave of fear that he had was washed away. He thought back to when they first started dating, how Shinee would not even dare to hold his hand when they were in public. Taeyang looked at Shinee as she gently caressed his entwined hand within her own, seeing her eyes soften.

"Thank you, for loving me. For being my best present in every way, everyday."

Now it was Shinee's turn to try and hide her flushed cheeks.

"We have to get to our seats before my fave takes the stage!"

Shinee gripped his hand tighter as she led them inside the venue.

This concert may have been Taeyang's Christmas gift to Shinee, but after an hour or so, even he had to admit that the artists and bands that have taken the stage so far were great to listen to. Each band had their own style, each artist had their own unique blend of sound, and he was finally able to see and hear why Shinee loved attending these events.

And to think, she would only go to these shows alone. For fear of sharing this part of herself with someone else and making them uncomfortable. He thought sadly.

Thinking back to weeks ago, when he gave her the concert tickets as a gift, Taeyang knew that day would be one he would not soon forget.

They meet at a new cafe near his home and Taeyang couldn't hide his excitement about the neon green box that Shinee had with her. Only when they had finished their drinks did she finally let him tear the wrapping paper off it. "Shinee! These are so cool - thank you!"

He grinned widely while staring at the new pair of trainers. Looking around the cafe to make sure everyone inside were busy looking elsewhere, he quickly tried them on and was surprised yet again.

"The guys that you play basketball with told me your size. After I privately messaged a few of them and explained why I wanted to know." She admitted sheepishly in Korean.

Shinee then pulled out a scroll of paper, but before she gave it to him, Taeyang noticed that her hands shook a little.

"If you don't like it, it's okay. I-I just wanted to show you what I see when you look at me is all."

Taeyang took the scroll from her, untied the silver ribbon, and stared.

It was a sketch portrait of him. The details that were etched on the paper were breathtaking.

"Really, it's okay if you don't like it. I can jus-"

As she reached out to take back the picture, Taeyang's hand touched the top of hers.

"No. This is my gift. I love it." he said proudly.

The uncertainty was in her eyes before she said otherwise. "Really? You really like it?"

Taeyang stared at her once more before looking at the drawing again. He could see the intensity in his eyes. As well as the tilt of his head and the cupid's inviting bow on his lips.

My butterfly saw all this? And was able to showcase it so well on paper? I guess my heart truly cannot hide its thoughts.

He then rolled back up the portrait and placed the ribbon back on it for safekeeping. "Yes. Thank you, my sweet butterfly."

As soon as we move into our honeymoon home, it will be the first picture that we frame together.

The thought entered his mind before he had time to intercept it, and in that moment he knew what he wanted - needed to do.

Wordlessly, he took out the envelope that enclosed the concert tickets in it. "I remember you telling me about this event months ago, and I wanted to experience it with you. I hope you do not mind."

What he really had hoped was that Shinee did not already buy a ticket for this concert to go alone, but once she opened the envelope and started squealing, Taeyang felt more confident that she had not.

"The Chill Jazz Seoul Christmas Concert! Are you serious?!"

Her eyes twinkled as she stared at him and then the tickets. "You really don't have to do this for me. I know that these concerts aren't your scene and I totally understand if you don't want to go." she offered politely in Korean.

Taking her hand into his, Taeyang spoke again, this time in English. "I want to. Really."

Shinee bit her lip and nodded before smiling up at him. "Then I cannot wait to experience this with you on Christmas day."

Being at this concert, with the woman that he loved, heart and all, Taeyang truly felt at peace. The next performer walked across the stage to begin his set and he could see Shinee trying to remember how to breathe.

"It's him! Oh my goodness - I finally get to see my favorite crooner in Seoul perform live!"

Her excitement was so infectious that even though Taeyang did not know who the performer was, he became excited to hear him sing with his band. Once the first few notes of the band played out, Taeyang closed his eyes and started to sway. *Whoa! This guy is pretty good.*

The sounds were a little dated, but they blended well together with the performer's voice.

Some time into the set, the music began to swell and fall in perfect time before the song changed to a more mellow and upbeat sound. Taeyang opened his eyes to see Shinee staring at him. Her smile made his heart sing, and he knew. *Now. I have to ask her.*

He took the small box out of his breast pocket and put it into his pants pocket. Without a word, Taeyang took Shinee's hand into his before he spun her around. He heard her gasp as he confidently placed her back into his chest. With his arms around her, Taeyang gently rocked the two of them from side to side as the music continued to play.

"You came into my life three years ago, and I have never been happier. Which is why I want you to stay by my side. For the rest of our lives."

Reaching down into his pocket, he took out the box and placed it in front of Shinee as she finally turned around to face him.

"Will you marry me?"

As he opened the box, Taeyang saw the unshed tears in her eyes and started to get down on one knee before Shinee wrapped her arms around him instead. Taeyang heard the song change to a more simple and softer piano melody as Shinee hugged him tighter. Pulling away slightly to see her face, Taeyang could see the freshly fallen tears that stained her cheeks. He brushed the others that came afterwards away as he asked her gently. "Is that a yes, my butterfly?"

Shinee nodded. "Yes! I want to spend the rest of my life with you too."

He embraced her again before placing the oval blue emerald ring onto Shinee's left ring finger and kissed her hand gently. " You are my never ending sunshine. Everyday and in every way. I love you Taeyang."

Before he could say another word, Shinee pulled him closer and kissed him deeply.

When the two parted, Taeyang caressed her face with both of his hands and looked at the ring now securely on her hand before gazing lovingly at the woman who now had his whole heart.

"I love you too."

• • ♋ • •

FALL IN LOVE WITH SNIPPETS of Shinee and Taeyang's love story from the beginning by joining The Stories Stations Playlists, K. McCoy's sweet and steamy community over on REAM Stories and Patreon today!

The Smallest of Gifts

The Winter season has become globally recognized as a time where loved ones are known for coming together in celebration of all that they have to be thankful for during the year with hopes of more to come.

Though for a few people, this time of year comes with a sense of obligation to spend time with others when they would much rather not.

How do you tell the ones you love that you would prefer to be alone during December without crushing their spirits like a fallen ornament to the ground?

This story explores that question, and shows that when you have people in your life who accept you completely as you are, that love and joy of the season can be felt no matter where, or how you chose to spend the season.

Chapter One
The Hopeful Crowd

Watching as the people shuffled around her in the chilly afternoon weather while she took a sip of her warm honey and ginger tea, Jetti tried to stop the corners of her mouth from turning upward as she sat across from her lunch date, Ricardo, at the outdoor cafe.

The change in weather—from the crisp orange and brown leaves to soft white snow—was quite possibly her favorite time of the year since deciding to make Krakow, Poland, her home away from home two years ago.

After finishing up another productive lunch date, Jetti felt rejuvenated. *I cannot wait to see this finished product! I just know that it is going to be amazing when it goes to print next quarter*, she thought as she began to bounce her crossed leg excitedly at the table.

"You know, it has been a few weeks since you and Ximena have met to catch up, has it not?" he asked while finishing up his espresso. Ricardo then cradled the tiny cup into both of his calloused hands and carefully placed it back to rest on its matching serving plate before he continued, "We would love it if you stopped by our holiday party this weekend. You know what they say: the more, the merrier. Right?"

Jetti's foot halted mid-bounce, and she slowly brought it back to the ground after hearing the invite that she was hoping to avoid today. Seeing the hopefulness in Ricardo's eyes only made Jetti feel more like a grumpy Grinch as she began to turn down the offer. "Thanks, but I don't think that I would be good company this weekend."

Feeling the subtle glare from his sudden yet thorough assessment of her physical and overall presence, Jetti rushed to add, "And I really do need to recharge my social meter before the new year hits and we are all swamped with work again."

Jetti's smile did not quite reach her eyes, but Ricardo accepted it all the same. As the two slowly stood up from their table, Ricardo reached behind him and picked up his large work messenger bag. Peering at the bag for a second longer than Jetti thought was normal, her friend looked to be mulling a complex thought over in his head before turning his attention back to her with one of his classic Cheshire cat grins. *So, he is not going to keep trying to sway me into going to their party?* She asked herself hopefully.

"If you say so, mi amiga."

Hearing Ricardo speak again and confirming her last thought made Jetti's day even brighter. Once the bag was securely placed over his shoulder, Ricardo held out his arms and grinned again as Jetti lowered her eyes and timidly walked into his warm bear hug.

Slightly swaying before parting, he chuckled. "Well, should you change your mind, let me give you our new address. I do not want my Mrs. Claus to be cross with me this close to the big day and all."

Giggling in agreement, Jetti added, "I totally understand. We for sure would not want you to wake up with coal in your stocking this year."

They shared another laugh before Ricardo turned around the thick strap to his messenger bag and unzipped the opening. He reached inside and removed a round object wrapped in gold gift paper. She took the small package from him and began to gingerly remove the wrappings to reveal a shiny, clear bulb ornament with fine cursive script written in blue ink on each side. Jetti's name shimmered on one side while the other had the lovebirds' new home address written on it within a hand-painted, intricate border pattern. Raising a playful eyebrow his way, Jetti teasingly asked, "What is all this? Are you trying to secure your spot on Santa's 'Nice List' this year or what?"

"I told you, Ximena is really going all out this year for the holidays. She even took extra time off from her last assignment to make these invitational ornaments for everyone."

Hearing that news tugged at Jetti's heartstrings. *Ximena really wants me to be there.*

Seconds before she could tell Ricardo that she had changed her mind and would be happy to show up for their housewarming holiday party, images of everyone else there in the tiny space filled Jetti's thoughts. She imagined loud laughing, drinks flowing, and multiple eyes all staring at her minus a plus one. *No way! I cannot deal with that mess again. Sorry, Ximena, but I'm just not ready.*

Jetti could still recall the stares she saw in the mirror as the lights danced at rapid speed during her last work New Year's Eve party three years ago. She remembered a woman twice her age all but digging her talons into her husband's arm as she threw her head back and laughed with the other women from her creative marketing department. They pointed and shook their heads at Jetti when they thought she would not notice after she excused herself to refresh her drink.

But she did notice.

Because I do not want what they have, do they think that it is okay to behave this way behind my back?

Before she lost her temper—or her holiday bonus—Jetti tracked down her boss and after thanking him for the 'lovely evening,' made a note to start looking for a new job elsewhere as soon as possible. As luck would have it, her passport had arrived the next week, and she took it as a sign from the universe to finally start traveling around the world like she had always dreamed of when she was growing up. *No way can I continue to work around these people and pretend not to know what they really think of me. They must think that I am some freak to show up to a place like that without a partner, especially since everyone else there is romantically attached.*

After a few more months of biting her tongue and refusing to go to any other company gatherings, she had squirreled away a little more into her savings and purchased her first one-way ticket to Poland. Jetti had met Ximena at The Dark Elixir Coffee Shop soon after her arrival in Krakow, and the two had hit it off instantly!

Their shared passion, love of traveling, and encouraging others to see the world led them to work together on a small company's freelancing campaign that same year. Ricardo, that company's Public Relations Manager, was smitten with Ximena from day one, and Jetti worried his feelings for Ximena would soon affect their new work relationship. Over time, as she saw that they did not, her fears of working with more people who would only shun her privately were slowly swept away.

As much as she loved collaborating on projects with the two, she still struggled to accept their offers of going out to social events, so much so that she finally had to share with them what happened at her last company gathering. They understood, and the trio reached an agreement: they would only mention networking events to her, and if Jetti could attend, she would let them know. They never brought up the subject again, and Jetti was thankful for that. The holidays were now the one time a year where she could feel them wanting to invite her to non-work-related events, but the two never did.

Until now.

Jetti could feel her heart tighten while envisioning herself having to entertain the group of folks with her 'happily single routine.' She quickly shook the images out of her head before bringing her full attention back to Ricardo. *Seeing and catching up with Ximena will have to wait until the new year, I suppose.*

Trying to take the focus of the conversation off of her, Jetti held up her invitational ornament and tapped it gently with her index finger, watching it lightly twirl and shine from the tea lights surrounding the cafe. "I love this little guy! As soon as I get back to my place, I will make room for him on my tree."

She stared at Ricardo again, noting how his eyes softened as he looked at the ornament within her hand. *Ximena is never far from his thoughts. I am really happy for them.*

And Jetti meant it.

Just because she was happy not having a partner did not mean that Jetti wanted her friends to be without one in their lives.

"Please thank the missus for me. It really is a wonderful invitation," Jetti told Ricardo once more.

"I will, but you know you could tell her yourself in person. Just say that you will be at our house tomorrow and wear something glittery and super festive."

Of course he would not give up on me that easily. Not with the possibility of making Ximena happy on the line.

Jetti beamed up pleasantly at her friend.

"How about this? I promise to wear my best festive sweater when I call to send you two all of my love by video chat this weekend," Jetti replied.

Ricardo wrapped her up into another hug, this time kissing Jetti on her forehead before he let her go.

"Alright. You take care of yourself, okay?"

"Always," she replied before the two went their separate ways.

Before calling it a day, Jetti made sure to pick up some groceries on the way to her apartment.

With the biggest day of December only hours away, she knew that this weekend everything would be closed, and she needed to stock up for her action-packed streaming weekend. Taking the stairs two at a time, Jetti was almost breathless when she reached her apartment and let herself inside. After putting away her food and ordering her holiday evening meal from the new soul food restaurant in the neighborhood, Jetti showered and put on her favorite onesie.

Smiling and content to be alone in her cozy apartment, Jetti turned on the decorative lights covering her miniature tree and watched as hues of pink, gold, green, and blue lit up the walls. Remembering her gift from earlier, Jetti retrieved the tiny ornament, making sure to hang it with care just below the mahogany angel that sat on the top of the tree.

She stood back and looked at her tiny tree in awe. It is not the biggest or brightest, but as far as Jetti was concerned, it was just right for her. Feeling the need to share this moment with her online friends, Jetti took out her phone and snapped a picture to post to her favorite social media account. A short message was all that was needed in the caption, and it was all Jetti had time to type. The doorbell rang, and she suspected her food delivery was waiting for her on the other side."Great gifts do not need to be grand, for even the smallest ones can say so much. Thank you XR!"

Jetti spent the next few hours streaming her favorite seasonal movies and sipping mulled wine over her ever-so-yummy holiday mini-feast. Just as she began to turn off her laptop and call it a night, an idea came to her.

It had been some time since she had played it, but Jetti was sure that with a quick refresher, she still could remember the classics. Or at least Ximena's favorites. Making her way into her tiny bedroom, Jetti went to the closet and pulled a soft baby blue gig bag from the top shelf. "Well, hello there, Fretter. It has been far too long since our last session."

Sitting on her bed, Jetti unzipped the gig bag and saw that her cherry oak ukulele was just as fine as the day she bought it from Strings and Things. After a quick tuning, she strummed it lightly to check the sound. The stings echoed harmoniously throughout the room, putting a twinkle in Jetti's eyes. She was going to love this. Jetti just knew it!

Excitement shot from the crown of Jetti's head to the tips of her toes as she leaped from the edge of her bed and grabbed her laptop. While waiting for it to come back to life, she thought back to all the songs that Ximena would put on repeat last year when the two worked together on a new traveling apparel campaign. As her computer lit up, so did her eyes as she remembered one key detail from that time. *Oh, Dios mio! Almost all of those songs were in Spanish!*

Refusing to let a little language barrier stand in the way of her plan, Jetti logged in and quickly typed in the name of the first song that she could remember. As the soft strings and the performer's voice filled her room, the memories of that time spent working and getting to know her close friend and Ricardo kept her up practicing each song. Before long, Jetti could see the beginning of a new day outside her bedroom window. The warm orange and blush-like hues were steadily beginning to spread across the sky. Exhausted, she finally put down her ukulele to fully take in the view.

Jetti was so glad that she recorded the last few tracks before noticing this. She would be even happier to be able to share these cover songs with Ricardo and Ximena! Getting comfier in her bed, Jetti uploaded the recordings to her email account and sent them to Ximena's primary email address before shutting off her laptop again.

Before the sun had made its grand entrance from behind the clouds, Jetti's head had already made contact with her favorite fluffy pillow, and she grinned as she drifted off into a well-needed sleep.

Chapter Two
Those Serendipitous Surprises

Ximena felt as though she was walking on air. Her Saint Nick really made all this happen today, and Ximena could not be happier! She stared at Ricardo with adoring eyes as he ushered guests into their new home.

Thinking back to when they first met, she still could not believe how everything turned out now. She had almost missed this blessing. She was glad that Jetti had convinced her to stay in Poland and to give freelancing another try.

When Ximena first arrived in Krakow, everything was one big adventure after the next. Until she was unexpectedly let go from her job and then couldn't find work elsewhere. Her family back in the States, worried about her well-being, started to tell Ximena that maybe it was time to come home. All her friends were quick to remind her how the market for expats in the popular city was simply too saturated, but Ximena was not one to quit when things got tough. She decided to try her hand at freelancing with her digital art degree. When that did not work out as she had hoped, Ximena had to get real about her situation.

So, as she was sipping coffee on what she had thought would be her last visit to her favorite coffee shop, The Dark Elixir, Ximena fought the tears that threatened to fall. Why did things have to end this way for her?

Grabbing a napkin to catch a tear that was about to slip down her face, Ximena spotted Jetti.

It had been some time since she had seen another foreigner, and this woman's cherry and midnight-blue smattering of shoulder-length locs caught her eye. Ximena listened as the woman softly ordered her drink in Polish. Ximena hoped that the woman would have better luck in Poland than she had.

Getting up from her seat, Ximena reached to grab her bag. As she turned around, she found herself face to face with the stranger she had been admiring only moments ago. The two gasped, but when Jetti smiled at her, Ximena returned it in kind.

"Hola! Lo siento, señorita."

In Poland of all places, hearing her mother tongue was what set off the onset of tears that Ximena had managed to keep at bay all day. This stranger probably thought Ximena was crazy! Why was she crying over something like this anyway?

Instead of leaving her in the middle of her sob fest as expected, Ximena was shocked to feel soft, comforting hands rubbing in a circular motion in the middle of her back. "Was my Spanish that bad?"

Ximena opened her eyes and found this stranger's kind ones staring back at her, with a tiny smirk pulling at the corners of her lips. Seeing this made Ximena smile again. She cleared her throat and spoke, "No, your Spanish was not too bad. But your Polish..." Seeing the woman giggle made Ximena laugh as well.

"My name is Jetti," the woman introduced herself.

"Ximena. It's nice to meet you."

"You too, Ximena. Are you leaving now, or can I join you?" Jetti asked.

If she only knew, Ximena thought to herself. She then remembered her landlord had said that they would not be able to pick up her keys until later that afternoon. Ximena reminded herself that she could stay a little longer before answering Jetti. "I can join you for tea."

The two talked over tea and tears, and along the way, they became the best of friends. Combining their talents and connections in a country far away from their homes, Ximena and Jetti became known as the freelance travel media tag team, the ones everyone wanted to work with in Krakow. Then came her insanely charming Ricardo, and soon so much more. Gently caressing her stomach, Ximena thought her heart would burst from the news she received during her doctor's visit yesterday.

I can not wait to tell him the news tonight!

She was so caught up in how she wanted to share the news with Ricardo, she was surprised when her husband casually strolled up behind her and wrapped her into his embrace. "I would love to know what you were thinking about just now. Everyone says that you are just giddy with the holiday spirit, but I know you, my gordita. What is really on your mind?" Ricardo asked.

Ximena leaned into his chest and smiled. "I was thinking about you and how we got here."

Not easily convinced, Ricardo pressed on further. "Really? Is that all that is on your mind?"

Of course he knows there is more. I did not marry him just for his good looks, Ximena thought while shaking her head. "I was also thinking of our work wife." Ximena sighed. "Before making her invitation, I prayed that she would say 'yes.' But it seems that I got all the miracles I was allowed this year."

Feeling her husband kiss the top of her head as the two swayed back and forth slightly, Ximena closed her eyes and listened to Ricardo's rich tenor voice vibrate soothingly against her back.

"I tried. And for a second, after I gave her the ornament, I thought we had succeeded in getting her to come today. But you know how she feels about these kinds of get-togethers."

Ximena squinted, and heat flooded her nostrils as she thought about what Jetti told them a year ago.

"I wish I could have seen those hyenas myself! Making Jetti feel like crap because she is happy and unattached. I would waste no time at all clawing out each of their eyes—"

Hearing Ricardo's chuckle caused Ximena to stop talking as she pulled away to look up at him. "Just what is so funny?" she demanded.

Ricardo tried to bring her back into his arms, but she swatted him away and pouted.

"You say that every time this topic comes up, so much that Jetti can mimic your little speech from memory by now."

Arching an eyebrow at this new information, Ximena stared hard at her husband. "So, you and Jetti mimic me during your little work lunches? I knew that I should have gone with you this time! I know for sure that she would be here right now if I had."

Imagining Jetti chatting and laughing merrily with others interrupted Ximena's mini-rant. Ricardo must have known where her mind went to as he took her hands into his, kissing each of them gently.

"It is okay. She is okay. I promise," he reassured her.

Not trusting herself to speak as she now felt both her nose and throat begin to sting, Ximena only nodded.

"Hija! Hija!"

Ximena could make out her mother's shrill voice anywhere and almost hid behind Ricardo from the sound. Before she got the chance to try, her mother quickly approached them, waving her phone in the air.

"Your phone is buzzing! Oh, Dios! Just who do you work for that would call you on this day? It is not right, hija!"

Taking her phone, Ximena began to check her messages with Ricardo looking over her shoulder.

"It is from the wifey! Open it already!" Ricardo urged her.

Ximena clicked on the message, and as they read the email together, she could feel her tears threaten to fall once more. *That Jetti! Always doing something to make me cry!*

"What does she mean, 'The Spicy Special Seasonal Mix'?" Ricardo asked with a smirk.

Ximena tried not to cry and laugh all at once as the two found space on their couch to sit. "I almost forgot about that," she replied.

Clearly not satisfied with her answer, Ricardo tilted his head, so Ximena explained, "Last year, when we worked on the Travel Chic Coolest Campaign, I was feeling super homesick and created a playlist of all my favorite holiday songs. Jetti must have remembered. Now that I think of it, how could she not? I played that playlist almost all day, every day for a week straight."

And she never once complained. Ximena thought back to that time and beamed at those memories. She and Jetti worked around the clock while everyone else was away visiting loved ones. They had food delivered, and Ricardo would show up, cracking jokes as he checked up on them to make sure they were still eating and resting when they needed to.

Looking at him fondly, Ximena let a tear slip from the corner of her eye.

That was when I started falling for him, she silently admitted.

"Well, if you are already crying, we should watch these clips, huh?" Ricardo joked.

Ximena nodded and pressed play on the first video. The two held each other close as Jetti's face showed up on the screen, with the ukulele Ricardo had talked her into buying a year ago.

Hola mi amors!

Thank you, Ximena, for such a thoughtful gift.

After I got home, I realized that I did not get you two anything this year. And I know that if I called you right now and said that, you two would say something oh-so cheesy about how I do not have to give you anything.

They continued to watch the screen as Jetti straightened her back and started to mimic Ximena.

You give me the gift of friendship all year; what else could I possibly accept better than that? How did I do that time, Ricardo?

Ximena saw Ricardo doing his best not to laugh as the video continued.

So please accept these performances, from the bottom of my heart to both of yours.

Thank you for being my friends, the best colleagues ever, and just the most all-around awesome people that a girl like me could ever ask to have in my life.

I love you both.

Happy Holidays!

The first chords were a little slower than the original, but hearing Jetti singing with her whole heart in Spanish, Ximena's all-time favorite song warmed her inside and out. This time, she did not bother with wiping her face as the tears fell quickly. The room grew quiet, and the sound from her phone was heard by more people than just her and Ricardo.

"Hija! Who is that singing?" Her mother asked as she stepped around a few guests to get closer.

"My best friend, the one I told you about earlier," Ximena answered, not taking her eyes off of her phone screen.

"Hmmm. She is not too bad. Hija, you have to help her with her R's some time! They are shaky."

Ricardo chuckled loudly, but Ximena was not sure if it was because of what her Mom had just said about Jetti's pronunciation or from the look on Jetti's face in the video after belting out her grito at the end of the upbeat Classic that she chose to cover from Ximena's playlist.

Either way, more people were making their way over to the sound, and soon there was a crowd in front of the two of them, clearly interested in what they were watching on her phone. Before they pressed play on the next clip, Ricardo looked out into the crowd.

"Does anyone know how to connect this phone to the flat screen?"

A few minutes later, the entire house was filled with the sound of Jetti's happy singing and strumming to several more seasonal songs. Some folks were even dancing, while the others simply nodded their heads along as they watched her perform in her bedroom on the couple's TV screen.

Ximena sat on the couch next to her husband, watching the scene around her. She tried to remember the last time she felt so much joy all at once.

Feeling a soft vibration on the couch, Ximena looked at Ricardo as he took his phone out of the back of his jean pocket and looked at the incoming message.

"Our Jetti did not want me to feel left out, I suppose."

Curious, Ximena leaned over to look at the message and broke out into the biggest smile ever.

Thank you for loving my best friend.

I think back to when we first met you, and I honestly cannot think of a better man to walk this life's journey with her.

I wanted you to know that I almost said yes when you invited me to the party yesterday. Someday I will, but for now, I want to thank you from the bottom of my heart for accepting and respecting my choice to say no.

Also, I did some online shopping when I woke up this afternoon and thought that I should get you something super fancy.

"Our Jetti is really something else! I have been waiting to try this cologne for a while now. How did she know?"

Ximena saw Ricardo scroll down on his phone to a picture of *Into the Wild*, a well-packaged cologne noted for being full of an earthy yet bittersweet smell. She tried not to let her mind wander recklessly about how delectable he would smell with a splash or two of it on his deep caramel skin when it arrived after the holidays.

Now is not the time for those thoughts, and you know it, hotpants! Especially not with your Mom in the room anyway, Ximena chided herself.

Ricardo kissed her cheek, ridding Ximena of her latest thought.

"She could not resist, could she?"

"Curious," Ximena asked. "What? Is there more?"

Her husband nodded. "For you, not me." Ricardo handed her his phone and kissed her check as Ximena read the last message from Jetti.

I saw these and just had to buy two pairs; one for me and the other for Ximena. Do you think she will like them?

Ximena stared at the pair of simple yet chic gold hoop earrings that Jetti had bought and could not shake the feeling of blessed fate that came over her. *Screw timing. I will tell him now!* She decided. *There is no way I cannot. All the signs are here. Gold, Myrrh, and Frankincense?! What else could they mean?*

The name was out of her mouth before Ximena could stop herself. "Jesus!"

Ricardo looked at her and laughed. "Come on, Ximena. I know that you are trying to cut back on all your cursing, but do you have to throw His name out in vain right now?"

Ximena shook her head as she stared at her husband, more tears welling up in her eyes. "No, I didn't mean it like that," she said with a calmness that she had never heard in her own voice before.

"Jesus... As in the name of our son." Thinking quickly, Ximena added. "Or Jesusa, if it turns out to be a girl instead?"

Seeing Ricardo stunned into silence, Ximena realized that he was starting to understand what she was trying to tell him.

"Are you saying, th-that you are... Really?"

When she nodded, Ricardo reached for her and pulled her close, covering Ximena in a quick session of sweet kisses, from the crown of her head to Ximena's cheeks before capturing her full lips.

"I knew that you were right about what you said earlier. We got all the miracles that we could have hoped for this year, my sweet gordita." Ricardo whispered gently against Ximena's ear. The two held each other close as they listened to Jetti sing with soft reverence. She gently finger picked the ukulele along to the ballad of how the one they were celebrating that day was brought into the world, and Ximena's heart was beyond full.

With her best friend, husband, and a new addition of love coming into their lives, Ximena knew that no other gifts would ever compare to the ones now etched into her heart.

Seasons of New Loves

P *eople are known to change, much like the seasons.*

Though just as seasons can be unpredictable at times, so can people.

Either of these sayings could be used to explain how Jetti Isley and Sebastian Gonalzes meet one fateful night.

This story follows the journey that Jetti begins, as her heart surprisingly makes room for someone other than her art, friends, and family. And continues with the start of Sebastian learning to curb his passions and the desire to lead with more than...his camera.

What will become of the inquisitive introvert and international playboy as their immediate feelings toward one another become more during the most wonderful time of the year?

Chapter One
A Chilly Reception

Jesusa cooed while reaching out to touch one of Jetti's brownish locs. At just five months old, the newborn had her Godmother wrapped around her finger. While staring down at her best friends' child, Jetti began to softly hum one of her favorite carols. She kept her eyes on Jesusa as she swayed the small child in her arms.

With Ximena and Ricardo entertaining their guests for another annual holiday party, Jetti was more than content to spend the night in the nursery. She expected that that was what the couple thought when they extended an invite to this year's party and Jetti wasn't upset in the slightest. Her love for small crowds hadn't faded, but over the last few months she found herself seeking out equally small opportunities to be more social.

If her two closest friends had noticed, they didn't show it. That only spurred Jetti on, knowing that she had found a community of chosen family that wouldn't judge her decision to keep her distance from the world when she deemed necessary. Some even sought her advice when it came to planning more future events thanks to the 'new normal' going on around the world. As Jetti had been practicing social distancing before it was mandatory, she expertly offered tips to her co-workers on how to connect with other folks without being physically close. Her creativity in and out of the office over the last two years seemed to have no limit, with more clients contacting her for freelancing projects.

As an Mixed Media Artist Specialist living abroad, Jetti Isley was in high demand in her home away from home, the small yet thriving town of Gdansk, Poland, And with her close friends only a short train ride away and the beach mere blocks from her residence, she couldn't dare ask for more.

A creaking sound interrupted her thoughts and Jetti looked up toward the door of the nursery. Seeing no one, she mentally dismissed the noise. *Maybe it was Ricardo checking in?*

Jesusa was Ricardo and Ximena's first child and the proud papa was still nervous about not being with the newborn at all times. Jetti didn't mind, as she loved seeing him dote on his daughter. *Yeah, he is for sure a girl dad.* She thought with a smile. No longer feeling the baby's gentle pull on her fluffy locs, Jetti looked down and her heart almost melted from the sight. Jesusa still held her hair within her tiny hand, but now the newborn's eyes were clearly losing the battle when it came to getting some sleep. When their eyes closed for a final time, Jetti gently removed Jesusa's hand from her hair and laid her into the crib. A yawn escaped her mouth and Jetti's smile widened at the cuteness before her.

Until she realized that with the baby down for the night, she had no reason to stay in the nursery. Looking back at the door, Jetti straightened her shoulders and took a deep breath. *It's okay, you can do this.*

Jetti knew that she could go out and mingle - in theory. That still didn't completely remove her apprehensions of all the possibilities of how wrong things could go. In small spaces and drinks flowy, she knew from experience how quick one well intended or malicious comment could put a halt to an okay mixer. For the last few months, she had gone out to one event each month, just to check her 'social meter'. Depending on the crowd and weather, she had no problem with staying out and chatting with others for an average of two hours. Even though Jetti knew that, something about this more intimate party put her on edge. *Jetti, go out there and be social.* She told herself. *If not for business, then for Ximena and Ricard. Afterward you can go home and stay up late binge watching the latest anime in your queue, okay?*

Before making her way to the door, Jetti turned to look at Jesusa one last and closed her eyes. The brightness from the many festive tea lights that adorned the living room took some getting used to, as she slowly opened her eyes.

There weren't as many people as she anticipated, and everyone seemed to be off in their own private conversations, with glasses of eggnog and apple cider in their hands. That made strolling around the flat much easier for Jetti. Though on her way to the patio, she noticed a woman alone, looking at the photos that were surrounding the large wreath with twinkling lights wrapped around it. She was about the same height as Jetti, maybe an inch or two taller, and her various shades of purple and blue twists reminded Jetti of her earlier years of being in Poland.

The woman must have felt her staring, because soon her eyes were on Jetti's. A small smile that didn't quite reach her eyes appeared on the woman's face and she offered Jetti a slight nod before returning to looking at the photos. Maybe it was the fact that the woman didn't make a beeline for her that held Jetti's attention, but she felt drawn to the woman in front of her. Soon Jetti's feet were walking toward her, stopping just a meter or so. A voice that she almost didn't recognize spoke, "I'm Jetti."

Jetti watched as the woman then turned around and sent another smile her way. "Nice to meet you. Both Ximena and Ricardo have said nothing but nice things about you. I'm Tasha, but my friends call me Tash."

Hearing Ximena and Ricardo's names put her more at ease. Inching closer, Jetti asked, "Are you new in the city?"

Tasha nodded. "I'm one of the new photographers for the YinYang Coworks relaunch."

Jetti had heard about the company YinYang from Ximena and was surprised that they'd hired a Black woman to help with the relaunching of their co-working space. From what Ximena shared, the company didn't seem all that diverse. *Maybe they're doing more than just relaunching the building this time around.* She wondered.

Tasha's soft chuckle ranged out in the otherwise quiet space. "You look like I did after doing my research on YinYang."

Looking at Tasha again, Jetti started to explain herself, but Tasha waved her hand between the two of them, "I was just as shocked after leaving Argentina for this assignment. But so far, the company has been real chill. No one has tried to touch my hair at all, or questioned my skills with my cameras."

Despite herself, Jetti found herself fighting back laughter. Just about every meeting she attended during her first year as a full time freelancer was full of those types of issues. It was what she now called her 'peak anxiety season' - pulling double duty between finding innovative ways to show potential companies her skill sets and creativity, while somehow professionally not losing her cool when those within said companies challenged her intelligent and personal space on a daily basis.

"Oh God! How I do not miss those days." Jetti blurted out. "I found myself going back to my place after work wondering why I don't just pack it all up and go back to the States."

Tasha's grin widened as she agreed. "In Argentina I had a few moments that made me ask myself the same thing. But what can I say? I'm too good at what I do to let a few bitter Becky's and Karens keep me down."

"You forgot about them Chaotic Chads too." Jetti added, causing Tasha to snort.

Smiling at Tasha's openness, Jetti stepped a little closer. "Luckily I met my friends here before one of them drove me to buy a plane ticket back home. I thou-"

"There you are, my sweet!"

The eye roll from Tasha set off the impending dread that started to settle into Jetti's stomach.

"Well, well, I see you have made the acquiesce of my latest muse."

Jetti's eyebrows knitted together as the man spoke again.

"My name is Sebastian, and I must say, you are even more beautiful up close." Extending his hand, Sebastian found nothing but cold air surrounding it, as Jetti chose to keep her hands to herself. "And may I ask your name?"

From the way his light brown eyes danced while taking in her figure, Jetti knew that the last thing she wanted to do was give him anything - especially her name. Reminding herself of where she was and why, she forced a tight smile onto her face. "You may ask, but I have no intention of giving it."

Hearing Tasha snort again eased Jetti's nerves a bit. She looked over at her new friend and saw Tasha glaring at Sebastian. *He must be a co-worker she can't easily dismiss. So glad I don't have those problems anymore.*

Thinking that her shortness would be enough to get him to back off, Jetti began to turn toward Tasha and continue their conversation. Though this Sebastian must not have gotten the message, as he cleared his throat. "Ah, you wish to remain anonymous. I normally would welcome such teasing theratics, though a few of my new friends have sent me here to find your name."

"Just what are you talking about Sebastian? What friends?" Tasha demanded.

Sebastian titled his head toward the other side of the room and Jetti's uneasiness in being in his presence was kicked into high gear. A group of people were waving at them to come over as many others stared at the TV screen in the center of the living room. She could see photos of herself as she held Jesusa on the screen. When one disappeared, another photo took its place - one after another. Panic rapidly found a home in the center of her chest and all Jetti wanted was to find a quiet place to hide.

Feeling someone enclose their hand into hers, Jetti blinked several times and saw Tasha standing next to her. "What in the actual hell is wrong with you Sebastian?! You seriously out here taking folk's photos without their permission?"

As he smiled, Jetti could feel her skin crawl.

"My sweet, it was all in good fun. I only wanted to show off my new DSLR for the others at YinYang." Sebastian explained.

She wasn't sure if it was the calm and confident manner in which he spoke, or the fact that the group of people were now making their way over to them, but Jetti found herself squaring up to the taller man. "In showing off your new gadget, you also validated my privacy. And now you stand here looking for a reward? Go to hell."

Managing to keep her voice to a harsh whisper, she was afraid that Sebastian wouldn't be able to hear her. Though Jetti watched as his smile flatlined just before Tasha led her away from the others and into the nearest room. As the kitchen door closed behind them, Jetti saw Ximena and Ricardo chatting on the phone. Her eyes betrayed her further, turning red at the sight of them.

"Mama, we have to go. I love you." Ximena said before ending the call. When she did, both her and her husband made their way to Jetti.

Ricardo reached Jetti first, standing in front of her as Ximena went to her side. "What is it amiga? Are you hurt?"

She was, but couldn't put into words how for fear of choking on the tears that threaten to leave her eyes. Luckily Tasha was still in the room and tried to explain. "One of the guests, a colleague of mine, unfortunately, decided to show his ass. In the process, he upset Jetti."

The feel of Ximena's hands rubbing small circles in the center of her back began to push away the panic that was trying to consume her. Taking a few short breaths, Jetti whispered. "I'm o-okay. Now, I'm okay."

"What is this guest's name?"

The steel-like tone coming from Ricardo was rare to hear. So much so that if she hadn't looked up when he spoke Jetti wouldn't have believed it came from him at all. She looked over at Tasha who met Ricardo's stare.

"Sebastian. Sebastian Gonzales."

Ricardo glanced at each of the women in the room, only pausing to scan Jetti over to see if she was truly alright. "Stay here. I'll be sure to escort this Gonzales out."

As the kitchen door opened and closed for a second time, Jetti slowly brought her eyes up to find Tasha and Ximena both looking her over. "I promise, I am better now." Jetti said.

Tasha let go of her hand and Ximena led Jetti to one of the barstools. "Let me get you something to drink. Do you want your favorite tea?"

Jetti nodded.

"Again, I apologize on behalf of my co-worker. I still can't believe he would think that that was a great conversation starter." Tasha offered.

Looking over to Tasha, Jetti nodded again. She thought back to the moments before the incident, how she really enjoyed talking with Tasha. A question formed in her mind and before her nerves got the better of her, Jetti asked, "Do you like coffee or tea?"

Ximena arched an eyebrow at Jetti as they waited for Tasha to answer the question. "Umm, tea? I like tea."

"I don't know how long you'll be in town for, but I enjoyed talking with you today. Can we meet again? Sometime next week?"

Tasha's smile slowly spread across her face. "Yeah. Let me give you my cell number right quick."

Jetti felt Ximena nudge her side, getting her to look up. Her eyes softened and the two leaned in closer as Tasha reached into her messenger bag. "Here's my business card. Call me anytime."

When Tasha handed Jetti her card, the kitchen door opened again as Ricardo marched back in. Tasha met him in the middle of the small space. "Again, I'm sorry about my friend. We've been working together for about a year now, but I never thought he would be so.."

Ricardo looked over Tasha to Jetti and Ximena, and Jetti smiled. Seeing this, he directed his attention back to Tasha, "...as soon as I can, I'll let him know how out of pocket he was tonight."

Instead of interrupting Tasha, Ricardo embraced her in a tight hug. She gasped and Ricardo swayed the two of them for a moment before letting go. "Thank you. And thank you for looking out for my amiga."

"I-it was no problem." Tasha spurted out. "I'm going to head out for the night. Thank you both for inviting me."

The trio watched as Tasha made her way out of the kitchen before Ricard spoke, "That was your first time meeting Tasha, Jetti?" When she nodded, Ricardo laughed."I like her."

Ximena reached out her arms and wrapped them around Jetti, adding a soft peck to her cheek. "Thank you for looking after Jesusa tonight. And it looks like you even made a new friend, despite that el pelmazo putting you on the spot like that."

"Good thing I never have to see him again." Jetti said.

• • ᴄᴚᴸᴬ • •

IT WAS THE MIDDLE OF the work week and Tasha's fitness tracker watch buzzed. She looked down and saw her lunch break reminder and quickly began putting away her laptop. After being in two hour long meetings, editing, and returning emails for the last five hours, she was more than ready for her lunch break. Getting to spend the next 90 minutes with a new friend was the icing on the cake.

Jetti called her over the weekend, and after chatting for a few minutes the two realized that they lived only a few blocks away from one another - Tasha in her employee flat and Jetti in a small house near the beach in Gdansk.

So they agreed to meet up for coffee that Monday, only to spend Tasha's entire break sharing their portfolios and favorite tracks from their playlists. When it was time to leave, Tasha asked if they could meet again tomorrow. And everyday that week, the two followed their new routine of going to Sol Cups for a quick sandwich, several cups of tea, and long conversations. It had been over a year since Tasha felt like she could talk to someone as freely as she did with Jetti, and she only hoped that she didn't burn out her social meter.

While they waited for their orders to be called, Tasha gently checked in with Jetti. "You sure you okay chatting up with me? I don't want to wear you down."

"Tash, it's okay. Spending time with you isn't taxing at all - I promise."

"Al Green! Green teas for Al Green!"

The duo looked at one another and burst into giggles as the name they put in for the order that day was called. "I'll get it." Tasha said, standing up to walk over to the pick up area.

Seeing the bista smile at her, Tasha returned it and picked up their club sandwiches and drinks. Something felt slightly off as she turned around to go back to the table, as if someone was watching her. Which wasn't uncommon, as for almost the last two years, Tasha became increasingly aware of her surroundings overseas, just as a precaution. Pausing, she scanned the cafe. Not seeing anything out of normal, she headed toward the table and placed the tray down before sitting. "So, did you hear back from that start up company that you were telling me about yesterday?"

After their lunch ended, Tasha and Jetti gave one another a hug and agreed to meet again tomorrow. Queuing up her playlist, Tasha got lost in the melodic yet upbeat sounds while walking back to the office. Though when she was a block away, her eyes narrowed in on the sight of Sebastain leaning against a lamp post. Much to her chagrin, the song ended and she could see his lips moving as she pressed stop on the phone. "Tash, could you please-"

"Only friends call me Tash. Go away."

Not breaking her stride, Tasha continued walking toward the office. Sebastian was in her face again. "Are we not friends? I still do not understand what I did to offend you so."

Taking out her fobs card, she held it up to the secured system that gave her entrance back into the office. "It wasn't me that you offended, and until you can figure out why I would be this way toward you, nah, I can't be your friend."

She heard him let out a heavy sigh and swiveled her neck. "Are you annoyed with me? Good. Then you know how I feel. Go try to impress somebody else with the latest gear in your grip cart - and while you at it- get a grip your damn self."

"Tasha, this is too much. How can I fix things between us, if I don't know what has occurred?"

Tasha rolled her eyes. Even when he was in the wrong, she couldn't deny to herself how fine he was. At five nine, he was a few inches taller than Tasha, with a cool ochre complexion that never failed to remind her of the sand along the beach of his hometown in Isla Verde. Several strands of his thick and shaggy curls shook loose, rushing to his forehead. The contrast coupled with his deep hazel eyes left Tasha staring at him a little longer than she intended too. *Nah sis - don't get caught up in his fioneness! He did Jetti dirty and needs to be checked.*

Tasha used her fob card again to let them into the second floor where they were working on the photos for the revamping of YinYang's Co-working space. With just three weeks left, she wanted to make sure that her photos were on point, so she looked behind her and stopped. "I know you have probably - definitely have been getting away with ignoring folk's boundaries because of your charms for years, but that stunt you pulled last weekend was rude as hell. Not to mention unprofessional as fuck."

"Must you use such language?" Sebastian asked.

Tasha continued, "Did you know who that woman was before you went into stealth mode with your new gear? Besides being a complete stranger to you, Jetti also happens to be good friends with Ricardo."

Sebastian's eyes widened and Tasha took a step back. "Do you mean Ricardo Ramierz - the marketing director for this project?"

"Glad to see you remember who has been signing our checks for the last month." Tasha snidely confirmed. "So the next time you try to be cute and photograph someone without their consent, think about that incident and put your camera away."

Seeing him thinking over her words, Tasha spoke again, this time without sarcasm. "If we're going to keep working together and be friends, you have got to promise not to pull another stunt like this, Sebastian."

"I didn't think...you are right Tasha."

He didn't let her speak another word, as Sebastian walked past her and sat at his desk. She looked at him, now lost in thought and hoped he was starting to get it together. Tasha had enjoyed working with Sebastian for the last year - the two completed their photography internship with Rebel Shots together and he was surprisingly an okay roommate during their time together in Argentina. But Tasha gave up too much back home to find herself caught up in his reckless behavior. If she had to choose between their friendship and her career, she wouldn't hesitate to cut him loose. *I hope you take my words to heart Sebastian.*

Chapter Two
Second Impressions and Chances

Her name is Jetti?

Sebastian sat at his workstation, repeating the name that Tasha let slip from her lips during their chat over and over in his head. He had seen her leave work again and since Tasha had been so cold to him all week, Sebastian thought he would get back in her good graces by treating her to something sweet.

There was a churro shop not too far away, and even though they didn't have cupcakes as she would have preferred, he thought she would appreciate the effort. But it was busy that day and catching up to her proved difficult as more and more people crowded the sidewalk and tram bus stops. A few blocks later it was him that was treated to the sight of seeing Tasha walking into a small cafe. Sebastian was about to walk up the small steps to go inside, until he saw the woman from the party. She had her hair up in a high bun and was wearing a scarf that was tied in the shape of a bow. *I know I didn't ask for anything this holiday season, but my my...how I would love to unwrap the gift that is this beauty.*

His thoughts were halted from going any further as he then caught a glimpse of Tasha looking around the coffee shop. Ducking to avoid her, Sebastian missed one of the steps and almost landed on the pavement. Two women walking by at the time glanced at him and giggled as she dazzled them with an apologetic smile. *I can't let her see me now - she'll be even more cross with me.*

Wanting to get another look at the other woman in the shop, Sebastian slowly rose from the steps and found her again, now laughing. Her smile seemed to light up the space, freezing him to the spot. He couldn't take his eyes off of her as she picked up her cup and sipped slowly before putting it down. *Those eyes...why do I feel as though one glance from them would leave me telling her all my secrets?*

He felt the same the night he captured her image at the holiday party. As he stood a meter away from the door, Sebastian got the composition he wanted with ease while focusing on her eyes. She was thinking about something and in that moment Sebastian wanted to know desperately what caused that light behind her eyes.

"Excuse us."

Turning around to the sound behind him, Sebastian saw three guys staring at him. With the steps to the coffee shop being so small, he realized that he was blocking anyone else from going inside.

"Oh, my apologies." He mumbled, lowering his head while stepping down. The men said nothing as they entered the shop, but Sebastian felt their glare all the same. Not ready to leave, he strolled across the street and busied himself with counting the tinsel adorned and bell shaped tree lights on each street lamp post. His hands began to feel the chill of the late afternoon weather, and since he was in a rush to catch Tasha at the office, Sebastian had forgotten to bring his leather gloves. So he stuck his hands into his jeans and looked back across the street, just in time to see Tasha outside. *I must find out her name, even at the risk of facing more of Tasha's wrath.*

She was one street behind him and while walking quickly, Sebastian watched Tasha slip on a pair of headphones. *Luck be a lady!* He thought excitedly. Sprinting down the street, he made it to the crossing before the light turned green. Once he was across the street, Sebastian used the few seconds left to catch his breath. The moment Tasha was within hearshot, he looked at her and quickly pleaded, "Tash, could you please-"

He wasn't surprised when she interrupted. In fact, Sebastian was prepared for it. *If she is talking, that would be my chance to find out why she is upset.*

The two had gotten to know one another well during their time together in Argentina, and one key thing he'd learned about her was that when she was crossed about something, her talking about the matter was a good thing. *That means it is something she is passionate about - that she thinks is worth seeing through.* If Tasha had ignored him and said nothing, Sebastian would have been worried.

So he did as little talking as possible, and it paid off. Sebastian had gotten the name he wanted, as well as the reasons why Tasha was behaving the way she was toward him. More employees came into YinYang, causing Sebastain to look Tasha's way again. Clicking away on her laptop, he took a moment to observe her and found himself smiling at the sight of her eyes focusing hard on her screen. Soon Tasha dropped her shoulders and rotated her head, in doing so her gaze landed on Sebastian. He continued smiling at her and his smile deeped when she sent one his way. *I have to fix things with Jetti. But how?*

. . ⚬⚮⚬ . .

THE NEXT DAY SEBASTIAN was a man on a mission. He took the morning off, choosing to spend that time researching all he could about Jetti. Not having much to go on, he began by looking into Ricardo. That led him to his wife Ximena's consultation business, where he was able to find Jetti's website. *Ah, she is a Mixed Media Artist? No one she gets along so well with Tasha.*

Soon his alarm went off, reminding Sebastian to get dressed. Once he left his flat, the next part of his mission began - returning to the place he saw Jetti last. He made sure to leave early enough to arrive before Tasha took her lunch and hoped that Jetti would be there. Walking inside the coffee shop, he didn't see either of them. Not wanting to give up just yet, Sebastian went to the counter and ordered an espresso before taking a seat with his drink at the same table that the two ladies sat at yesterday. While sipping the last of his drink, Sebastian finally sees Jetti walk in. Wearing a houndstooth jacket with a black boots and leggings, he watched as her hands went to the top button of her jacket. Sebastian's mind goes into a blur as everyone around her fades away and in slow motion she undoes two buttons, revealing a green blouse.

Jetti came to a stop mid way through the walk to the table and began to turn around. Standing up, Sebastian quickly left the table to make his way to her. "Please don't go. I - "

The frown on her face jarred his images of her from yesterday, and Sebastian lost his train of thought. "I, ah, was hoping to see you before you had lunch." He almost let out a sigh when she turned back to face him, until he noticed that her eyes now glared at him.

"No."

Taken aback, Sebastian almost didn't notice Jetti as she started to walk past him. He reached out for her wrist but flashes of Ricardo grabbing him in the same fashion while 'escorting' him from the holiday party made him pause. With his hand mid air, Sebastian looked on and watched Jetti sit down. *I only have a few minutes left.* He reminded himself.

Her eyes continued to glare at him as he returned to the table, sitting across from her.

"How did you know I was here? Why are you here?" Jetti asked, looking around rapidly.

This is my chance.

"I, um, saw Tasha leaving from this place yesterday. You too, so I had hoped you would be here today." he explained.

Seeing her shoulder raise slightly, Sebastian rushed out. "Tasha has been in rare form with her particular brand of duplicity, since the night we met. And I was hoping that perhaps meeting with you would help put an end to that."

"You wanted to see me to make things easier for you with your co-worker?"

He tried to read Jetti's face, but she remained stoic. "Well, yes, to start I suppose." he answered honestly.

Jetti looked at the entrance again and sighed. "I guess it would be a start." She continued. "Can I assume that Tasha doesn't know about your plan to show up here today?"

"Yes, that's -"

She cut him off. "Good. If I agree to meet you tomorrow, will you please leave?"

That was unexpected. He thought. Knowing that Tasha would be there any minute, Sebastian agreed. "Where shall we meet? How about for dinner at the bistro down the street?"

"Okay."

Jetti looked between him and the entrance. Standing up and grinning at a job well done, Sebastian picked up his empty cup and put one of his business cards on the table. "I look forward to seeing you in my dreams until then."

.. ⁓ ..

TO SAY THAT THIS DATE was not going as Sebastian envisioned it would have been the understatement of the year. He made sure to dress for the occasion, skipping a trip to the gym to shave and give himself a haircut. In his favorite pair of deep brown slacks, a beige turtleneck, and matching brown loafers, Sebastian managed to get the eye of everyone inside the Asian and Polish inspired fusion bistro. Everyone except the woman sitting across from him. From his careful assessment, it appeared that Jetti came to this place straight from work after she sent him a message saying she would be late.

He allowed himself to think that she was running late because of wanting to shower and change before meeting him, but seeing her in a pair of dark jeans, boots, and a white long sleeve top, Sebastian doubted that was the case. She didn't remove her mask until their food arrived, making small talk between them even more difficult, with the music and others around them chatting. *Surely she will warm up more once I show an interest in her work?*

"I visited your website earlier this week and must say - your unique blend of American, Spanish, and Polish content is quite impressive."

A small smile graced her lips, "Thank you."

It was the first time that evening that Jetti had looked at him directly, so Sebastian accepted it heartedly. "If you are ready, I can pay for our meal."

"No need. I frequent this establishment often enough to request my portion be placed onto my tab."

Sebastian lowered his head, attempting to hide his wounded pride. *That explains why she took longer than usual talking to the waiter.*

Reaching for the glass of water in front of him, Sebastian took a gulp and set it back down. "I see. Okay then, would you be willing to accompany me for a walk through the park? I hear that the tree lighting ceremony will be taking place there tonight."

"I would like that." Jetti said, now beaming across the table from him.

Leaving the bistro, Jetti kept her distance from him as the two walked outside. If anyone were to see them, it would be easy to assume that they were merely strangers sharing the sidewalk. That thought irritated Sebastian to no end, causing him to try and spark a conversation. "According to your website, you have called Poland your home for years now."

"Yes."

When will she say more than a few words to me? He wondered.

Fixing a tight smile on his face, Sebastian tried again. "And you seem to speak the language well. How is that?"

"I attended an intensive Polish language school."

Racking his brain to think of something else to say, Sebastian didn't notice as Jetti stopped walking. Turning around to find her there, he looked behind him to see her staring at him. "What were you hoping to achieve by seeing me this evening?"

It was a simple question, but the directness in which Jetti asked it caused him to think it over. Normally he didn't have to work this hard to be charming. Part of him wondered why he was even putting forth this much effort with her when he could have left her at the bistro and found someone more willing to welcome his advances. That was until he began to walk back to her and saw Jetti take two steps backwards. Her eyes were locked onto his, and Sebastian noticed that she was no longer wearing the mask that she put on after leaving the bistro.

"I feel that we may have gotten off to a more than troubling start. This is my way of fixing that."

Jetti continued to stare at him. "There is another way of doing that."

Grinning, Sebastian went to her again. "Well, in that case...we can skip the tree lighting and head back over to my place. It isn't far from here."

As she looked down, he closed the distance between them and waited for her to look up at him.

"Honest question - at the risk of sounding rude - what do you have to offer anyone? Besides what's in your pants?" Jetti stared at Sebastian as he coughed and quickly looked around the park.

Sebastian took his time returning her stare. "I thought that you..."

"What you thought was obvious, but what I was trying to say is a simple and sincere apology could have fixed what you called a 'troubling' start."

He watched as Jetti stepped further away and looked out past him. "I'm an introvert and also suffer from severe anxiety. For years now."

"I had no idea."

Jetti kept her gaze on the other passerbyers, sighing before she continued. "Years ago, in the States, I worked for a company where I thought people at least respected my preference to keep to myself, only to find out that they thought I was an undateable joke. That was the last corporate sector I worked in before coming to Poland and launching my freelance career."

She closed her eyes and Sebastian felt himself wanting to comfort her, but not sure how. Willing himself to stay still, he looked on as Jetti slowly opened her eyes and directed her gaze back to him. "Since then, I have made friends who don't make me feel bad for being the way I am

- they accept and love me like family. So, after years of them asking, I finally got enough courage to attend one of their holiday parties at their house last weekend."

Sebastian's face went hot as flashes of the photos he took that night entered his mind. Playing back the words she said to him that night followed ...*you also validated my privacy...go to hell...*

It was his turn to look away.

"It was the first private event I attended in five years and you left me wishing I had never gone at all. I think an apology is the least that would be due."

When Sebastian turned back around to face Jetti, he didn't say a word at the sight of her walking away.

* * ᴄᴂ * *

"SEBASTIAN? IS EVERYTHING okay?" Paul, one of the staff members at the office looked at him, concerned.

He wished he'd called in today, but since he took yesterday off, Sebastian didn't want anyone to think he was slacking off. "Of course, everything is great."

Paul looked him over again. "If you say so. It's just you haven't been your normal self today."

Plastering a smile to his face, Sebastian met the man's stare. "Thank you for your concern, but I am in good health." *That wasn't entirely a lie.*

Though he hardly got any sleep last night after meeting with Jetti. Her words were on repeat, along with the faraway look in her eyes as she told him about her condition. Now knowing more of the situation, he understood why Ricardo was quick to toss him out that night. *He was protecting his friend - from me.*

The need to make things right with Jetti grew more with every second Sebastian spent in the office that day. By the time the day was over, he was left alone in the office, staring at her number on his phone.

Thinking of how to reach out to her, instead of doing what he initially wanted and calling her directly, Sebastian went to his messages and sent her a brief text. When his phone buzzed, he quickly grabbed it, reading over her reply.

"Thank you for seeing me again today." Sebastian said to Jetti.

The two had agreed to meet at The Botanical Gardens, and he was surprised to say the least. As it was the end of the year, hardly nothing was in bloom and visitors were scarce.

"Well, you did send me a text, saying you would meet me wherever I wanted." Jetti replied.

Her arm brushed against Sebastian's, and the static electricity was enough to make its way up to his shoulder. He found himself looking forward to it happening again.

"I love coming here - anytime of the year. During the Spring, when all the flowers are blooming and even now, when the gardens are all but vacant."

Sebastian couldn't stop himself from asking, "But why? As you just said, nothing is in bloom. No beauty to be seen at all."

When Jetti's eyes landed on his, Sebastian realized that he had misspoke.

"There is beauty all around. You just have to look closely to find it." Jetti giggled. "And here I thought you would have known that, being a photographer and all."

How right you are, Jetti. There is so much beauty in this space right now.

His eyes were fixed on her, as Jetti led them to a nearby bench. Sebastian watched her remove her messenger bag from around her neck and reached inside, taking out a sketchpad. "I have to admit, I did have another reason for wanting to come here today."

"You did? May I ask what that reason is?"

Her eyes went from her sketchpad to Sebastian, and when Jetti's eyelashes fluttered before looking back down, his hand itched to lift her chin up to his eye level.

"I wanted to listen to your description of the gardens. I've been coming here for years and since it's my happy tank, I feel a bit biased in giving my opinion to a new client."

"A happy what?" he asked.

A soft chuckle escaped her lips and Sebastian briefly closed his eyes to enjoy the sound. "My happy tank. Here is where I spend most of my time, after meeting with clients, when I need to clear my thoughts or to find inspiration for a project, this is where I like to visit."

She opened her sketchpad and looked up at Sebastian. "So, would you be willing to share with me your thoughts of The Botanical Gardens? As a first time visitor?"

He made a show of looking at their surroundings, going as far as to stand out and walk in a tight circle before sitting back down. Jetti's chuckle turned into a full laugh as Sebastian spoke. "Well, at first glance, it is very quiet. Not many people spend time here, and that at first was a bit strange." With his eyes never leaving hers he continued. "Though the more time I am here, I can see that no matter the weather, the gardens have many charms waiting to be explored and appreciated."

Jetti's eyes widened briefly before she started to write onto her sketchpad. Sebastian looked on and saw that she was also drawing what looked like words floating into the air. Seeing her add lips to the pad, he bit into the corner of his. "I want to see you again." he blurted out.

Looking up for her work, Jetti blinked a few times and nodded.

"I-I would like to see you again too."

Chapter Three
The Holiday Surprises

Over the last week, Jetti found herself spending her days at work, lunch with Tasha, and more of her weekends exploring Poland with Sebastian.

Sharing this update with Ximena and Ricardo, the two had expressed their worries about her weekend 'outings' but once they could see that Jetti was fine they since have been teasing her about her 'full schedule'. As rough as her first introduction to Sebastian was, their time together since the Botanical Gardens trip had been great. Jetti found herself growing curious to learn more about him, which prompted her to want to spend time with him.

"So everything is still okay? With Sebastian, I mean." Tasha asked during their last lunch together.

Jetti tried not to blush, but she felt her cheeks grow warm all the same from the mention of him. The day before the two of them attended a pretzel baking class and Sebastian's eagerness to help left them covered in flour. If that had happened before, Jetti would have apologized profusely and quietly cleaned up the mess before making a dash out of the room. Instead, she looked at Sebastian, his hair completely coated white as he rubbed the back of his neck and cheeks. With more flour on his face, Jetti burst into giggles and Sebastian joined her. The two somehow managed to clean up their station and make a pretty decent pretzel.

"Good."

She hadn't answered Tasha's question outloud but the look on her face must have been enough assurance for her friend.

The following day she was going to meet Sebastian at a video arcade bar, but as she was heading home, he messaged her saying that he couldn't see her as planned. The heaviness in her chest was unexpected and Jetti stared at the message for longer than she meant to before responding. With nothing else to do, she considered going to the bar alone. *I want to see his reaction to the place first.*

With that thought, Jetti was left with no choice, at least to herself. *I like spending time with him.*

The small voice in her head was small, but she heard it. And couldn't disagree with it. Try as she may, Jetti was forming an attachment to Sebastian. He hadn't said the words yet, but his actions toward her over the last few weeks showed her that he was aware that what he did the night that they met was awful. He since then had been patient on their outings, making sure she was comfortable and clear in his words and actions. From respecting her personal space to listening to Jetti's thoughts about the topics they discussed, Sebastian was slowly winning her over.

He left her a voicemail, apologizing again for the late cancellation of their 'non date' and asked if they could meet today instead. And since she knew that there would be less people at the video arcade bar, Jetti agreed.

"I see you made it underground okay." Jetti said as Sebastian walked toward her down the narrow and dim stairway.

He glanced around the entrance to the bar and when she saw him smile, Jetti grabbed his hand. "Let's go inside."

They spent the night taking pictures inside with the older working arcade style games and playing with the dance games. After their last round of dancing, Jetti walked away from the floor and Sebastian followed her to the bar.

"I'm so tired! But I forgot how much fun this place was - thanks for agreeing to come out with me." Seeing him grin while looking at her, Jetti felt butterflies lift and take flight within her rib cage. It was slow at first, but the more Sebastian stared at her, the higher the butterflies rose, making it hard for her to breathe.

"Thank you for showing me around these last two weeks. I enjoyed it."

The sincerity in his voice left Jetti wanting to hear more. Biting the corner of her lip, she moved in closer so she wouldn't have to shout over the game theme music now playing inside the bar, "I'm glad. What kept you away yesterday?"

"Family back home. I almost forgot that I had a video chat scheduled yesterday with my mom."

Jetti was now at full attention. Over the last week, Sebastian spoke more and more about his family, especially his mom. She liked seeing how his eyes lit up when talking about her. So Jetti asked, "How does your mom feel about you not being home during this time of the year?"

Sebastian's eyes drifted away, not for too long, but Jetti noticed the change. His eyes lost a bit of their warmth too as he answered. "She would like me to be home more, though with the medical expenses that we have from her cancer treatments, she understands."

He hadn't shared that before.

She wanted to kick herself for asking about such a sensitive topic, but before she could apologize, Sebastian spoke again," She's been sick for some time now, and as the only one with a study income, I am taking whatever assignments I can while my older brother and wife stay home and care for her back in Puerto Rico."

"I understand. You don't have to talk about it more if you don't want to." Jetti told him.

Sebastian reached out and gently placed her hand into his. "Thank you. I feel better having told someone, so thank you for listening."

Jetti's butterflies now hammered within her chest, practically begging to be closer to Sebastian. The feeling was so rare that she hardly remembered the last time she felt it. As their eyes stayed on one another, she felt the pull to him. And for the first time, she didn't have a knee jerk reaction to get up and leave. She instead stared at Sebastian's lips and breathed deeply, closing the space between them. As she felt the haze around her lull her eyes close, Jetti heard Sebastian's voice again. "About the first night that we met. I want to apologize. It is my sincerest hope that you can accept my apology for ruining what was probably a great night for you. At least before I came along and made a mess of things."

With her heart making its way back to the center of her chest, Jetti had to remind herself to take slow breaths. "Thank you."

"I suppose we should go. It is getting late and I don't want you to miss the last train." Sebastian said.

He was right, but with the jolt of passion that now began to fan throughout her body, Jetti wanted to at least taste his lips, especially as they seem to call out to her. Wordlessly, Jetti stood from the bar stool and her legs slightly swayed when they touched the ground. She felt Sebastian reach out behind her, his hand to the small of her back. Closing her eyes to enjoy the feel of his sturdy arms holding her close, Jetti found herself at a loss for words. Just Sebastian being this close was wrecking her senses in the most wonderful of ways.

Her breathing was shallow, and she could only hope that Sebastian didn't notice. Softly blinking her eyes back open, Jetti found his warm gaze on her and it sent a pulse to every erogenous part of her being. Not trusting herself to speak when Sebastian released her, she chose to lead them out of the underground bar.

• • ⁙ • •

ANOTHER WEEK OF DATES passed and Sebatian's affections for Jetti continued to grow. With every outing, he was finding each of her quirks to be more charming than the last. The way she would greet people while they walked along the markets, and how the older people would use their limited English to engage in conversation with her left him speechless. He was all but forgotten sometimes, and Sebastian didn't mind. Being in the background allowed him the pleasure of seeing people's eyes sparkle when Jetti would politely reply to them in Polish.

Years ago, when he set out to make a living traveling with a camera, his mama told him a quote about how one can touch another's heart by speaking with care their mother tongue. At first Sebastian thought it was just mama's way of reminding him to be respectful of the people he would meet, but after having the privilege of seeing Jetti interact with the people in her small town, he finally understood what she was trying to tell him. *Sweet Jetti, thank you for letting me see the world through your eyes.*

With a week left in the year, Jetti would be spending her time with Ximena and Ricardo, so she invited him to visit her in Gdansk. Knowing that he might not have a chance to see her again, with their assignment ending soon at YinYang Coworks, Sebastian made sure to book a room in the city so he could go wherever she asked.

On their last day together, Jetti asked him to meet her at the beach. It was far too cold to go in for a swim, but once he realized how secluded the area would be this time of year, Sebastian knew why Jetti would want to go there. Making sure to dress for the warm weather, he left his hotel.

"Did you find it okay?" Jetti asked.

Sebastian didn't get a chance to answer before Jetti fell in step with him. Her hand brushed against his and he felt it warm for her brief touch. The two walked along the shore in silence, and he surprised himself by not feeling the need to fill the space with funny banter or a clever line that hinted at something more.

Thinking back to their first dinner together, Sebastian felt the waves of embarrassment overcome him. *How I almost missed my second chance at getting to know this woman beside me due to my own foolishness.*

He looked down at Jetti and marveled at her quiet independence. She didn't have on a mask, so Sebastian was able to take in her serene face, staring straight ahead while she walked beside him. Another wave, this time filled with misplaced pride he felt the night he invaded her privacy with the intimate portraits he took of her without permission. "I am truly sorry."

Jetti turned to face him, putting an end to their walk. "For what Sebastian?"

"That night we first met. I was completely captivated by you, and wanted to have a memento of you for myself that I used my profession to claim a private moment of yours."

She looked at him and then out to the beach.

"Thank you."

They stare at one another and Jetti spoke softly, "Your actions since that night have spoken far louder than any apology, but it's still nice to hear."

Sebastian set his jaw, the desire to caress Jetti's cheek, to breathe her in closer was taking over all his thoughts. And the longer he stared at her, the more his heart ached to touch her. Soon Jetti's face was inches away from his and Sebastian closed his eyes when her lips brushed against his cheek.

Seconds felt like minutes as Jetti took her time stepping away from Sebastian's face. "What are you doing this New Year's Eve?"

Sebastian smiled before reaching for Jetti's hand. Enclosing it within his, he lightly brushed his lips along her knuckles before answering, "That, my sweet Jetti, is completely up to you."

When she beamed up at him, Sebastian couldn't resist placing a kiss on her temple. He looked down and noticed that Jetti swayed slightly while fidgeting with the ends of her coat sleeve. "I was just wondering...but now..."

Hearing her voice flatter worried him, so he brought a hand out to gently rub the side of her right arm. "Whatever it is, you can tell me."

"I don't think I can give you what you want." Jetti whispered, "At least, not now."

Can she honestly not see? How what I have come to feel toward you is more than physical?

"That is good to know."

Sebastian didn't realize that he had spoken out loud, but was thankful that she knew his thoughts. He reached for Jetti's hands and caressed the inside of her palms, lightly tracing his fingertips over her knuckles. "Though over time, should you change your mind, I will follow your lead." Before she could say a word Sebastian continued, " But please know, you have already given me more than I had expected to receive. Thank you."

She rolled her eyes but Sebastian saw a soft smile grace her face as she began walking again along the beach, with his hand still entwined within hers.

This heartachingly sweet read features Jetti Isley, Ricardo and Ximena Ramierz from **The Smallest of Gifts.** *And Sebastian Gonzales, a new character found in K. McCoy's upcoming novel,* **Doves Cry Too**.

Find out more about the sizzling yet serious photographer by joining K. McCoy's newsletter. The Stories Stations today at www.authorkmccoy.com[1] !

---

1.   http://www.authorkmccoy.com

The Season's Many Blessings

Every holiday season comes with its challenges and surprises. How people choose to face things that test them has the potential to change who they are. As this is Tasha and Jerome's first year as husband and wife, they are determined to see every moment possible together.

Chapter One
Sweet Mornings

A year of marriage and Tasha still hardly believed that she was a married woman. Though her husband made sure to remind her every chance they got, and she had to thank the OG for that. Though at the moment she was a little bit preoccupied. Their breakfast sat on the kitchen island, growing cold. All because Tasha asked Jerome if there was anything else he wanted to eat before he blessed their meal. He had just gotten in from his morning workout and didn't bother with putting on nothing more than a pair of briefs after taking a shower. She watched him look up from his plate and that lopsided smirk was in full effect. *I know that look...*

Sure enough, Jerome stood. "Yeah. I think there is."

Already feeling her pulse pick up from his gaze, Tasha tried backing away. Looking at the clock on the microwave just behind Jerome's shoulder she let out a soft sigh and smiled, "Rome, don't start. We have a whole day of things to get done."

"And as long as you come first, everything else will get done."

Her heart and core both reacted in time to the low tone that left Jerome's lips. It had been almost a year and Tasha still clenched her thighs together when he talked to her like that. She didn't move as Jerome closed the distance between them. Jerome reached for her left hand and brought it to his lips. Turning it over, he brushed Tasha's fingertips across his lips. Getting a full view of thick chest and deep umber skin, Tasha began to welcome the change in their mornings plans. It was too easy to do, as their complexions almost blended together from the sunlight that crept in from the expansive windows inside their home.

Trying one last time to get him to at least eat some of the eggs, toast and bacon that she had made, Tasha spoke, "I know that, but what about your breakfast?"

Jerome looked Tasha over slowly, bringing her hand to his shoulder. "Oh, I intend to eat."

Tasha slowly shook her head and as his lips pressed against her forehead, she chuckled. Their eyes landed on one another before Jerome's hands began roaming over her body, starting at Tasha's sides. Jerome was in no hurry as he carried on with his exploration, stopping for a bit to give her shoulder a kiss. Even while wearing one of his old oversized t-shirts she felt the softness of his lips. She then brought their bodies closer, placing her other arm around his neck and the content groan he released made Tasha smile.

When his firm hands found her thighs, Jerome went to work on lifting up the shirt. Feeling a chill in the air as he brought the shirt over her soft stomach, Tasha put her hands up and closed her eyes. The edge of the shirt teased her nipples for a second and combined with not being able to see, only feeling Jerome's presence caused more moisture to gather in her waiting folds. Blinking slowly she re-opened her eyes and bit the corner of her lip at the sight of Jerome staring at her.

• • ❧ • •

A FLASHBACK OF THEIR first week as husband and wife played out in her mind, how even though Tasha was comfortable in her fuller figure, it still took many well placed kisses and affirmations of appreciation from Jerome before she was completely at ease in front of him naked. Now down to just a pair of panties, Tasha stepped toward Jerome again, sighing heavily from the contact of their bodies together while wrapping her arms around his neck. "Rome..." she whispered close to his ear.

Her feet no longer touched the ground as Jerome lifted her up. "My god, you are beautiful."

With the smell of her want for him steep in the air, Jerome inhaled deeply and took his time exhaling. Tasha could feel his dick near her entrance and her need to have him fill her sent Tasha's hips rocking.

Jerome gritted his teeth before stilling her movement with a kiss on the lips.

"I thought you wanted me to eat first." he reminded Tasha as he went back in for another kiss.

A whimper almost left her lips when he tried to pull away, but Tasha's hands were quicker. With them now securely behind Jerome's head, she brought their lips together once more. Her tongue went in search of his and as they touched, Jerome's knees swayed for a second. The room spun when Jerome turned around and sat Tasha on the kitchen counter. The coolness of the countertop was a contrast to how she felt, shocking her into pulling her lips away from Jerome's.

He didn't take his eyes off of hers when he dragged both arms down back to sides, pausing once they rested on Tasha's hips. Jerome hooked his hands inside the waistband of her fabric and tugged until her panties came down over her stomach. Leaning back and lifting up her lower half, Tasha looked on as he brought her panties past her thighs.

"Look at you." Jerome whispered, bringing more heat to Tasha's face.

The way he glanced at her, fully nude, made even more want pulse down to her slick folds. She felt like a work of art in his presence. And it was clear how much he cherished every inch of Tasha, all the way from the crown of her head to her toes.

She wanted nothing more than to be with him, but one thing about her husband was that he was one to take his time in making sure things were done well. Especially when it came to things that mattered. So Tasha willed herself to not rush the experience. Bringing her lips together in anticipation, she watched Jerome trail his hands lazily along her thighs. He placed both hands onto her knees and slowly spread them apart. As he did, the wet sounds from below followed, almost tempting him closer.

Instead, Jerome used Tasha's legs to bring her closer to the edge of the countertop, prompting her to use her hands and elbows to study herself. She had to remind herself to breathe when Jerome lowered himself in front of her warmth. Alternating kisses from the beginning of her thighs, starting from the back of her right knee, Jerome sent small smacking kisses lower and lower, until his nose brushed against Tasha's mound.

Pushing her moist folds open with the tip of his tongue, a long moan escaped her lips. One steady flick after another, Tasha's thighs were trembling as she reached out a hand to guide Jerome deeper to her sweet spot. Just as she rubbed the crown of his head, Jerome flattened his tongue, firmly teasing her pulsing pearl. "Oh-OH! Rome, I-"

Tasha's legs trapped Jerome in place when sweet nirvana took flight throughout her body. But Jerome didn't seem to have any intentions on breaking free of her hold, instead he hooked his arms around Tasha's thighs and pulled her closer. The hand she had brought forward was now trying to break free of the pleasure he was delivering. *It's too much - I can't take it.*

With her eyes tightly shut as Tasha rode one more wave of unique passion, she felt Jerome finally release his hold, letting her legs fall. Slowly she blinked her eyes open to find Jerome staring at her. His gaze told her at that moment that he was far from done. Breathing heavily, Tasha stared at her juices glistening around Jerome's mouth and chin, and she leaned forward to get a taste. Starting at the bottom of his chin, Tasha licked her essence off of him. The aroma of his spicy citrus and sage combined with her tart sweetness had her throbbing at her core again.

His breathing hitched when she made it to his mouth, but Jerome didn't move. Though the moment their lips touched, he gripped her tightly into his arms. Needing to be closer to him, Tasha wrapped her legs around his waist again. "Rome...please- I-I-"

She felt the cold breeze on the bottom of her ass as Jerome picked her up from the counter and closed her eyes while holding on to him for dear life. Splaying her hands across Jerome's back, Tasha felt his muscles constrict and expand and she pressed into them. Tasha wanted to see him, to see the want in his eyes for her, so she opened her eyes in time to Jerome sitting down on the edge of their couch. She only got a glimpse of the hunger in his irises before Jerome aligned himself to her entrance and without a word entered her heat.

"Damn, Tash..." Jerome groaned in between thrusts. "You so wet."

The fact that her husband only cussed when he was deep inside her warmth made Tasha even hotter. She clung to him, mouth slightly open from the pleasure that Jerome's swift strokes gave her as they made love. Their pants and moans echoed throughout the house as the sun filly rose and Tasha was ready to stay in this way for the rest of day, if it meant more loving like this.

Jerome stroked the sweet spot inside her walls and Tasha dug her nails into his lower back. "Ah, Rome! Again!" she cried out while dragging her hands up to wrap around Jerome's neck.

He did as she asked and Tasha arched her back in appreciation. Jerome then bent his head downward and latched his lips onto her neck, sucking firming against her deep brown skin. Tasha extended her neck as far as possible, wanting Jerome to mark her as his. A smacking sound echoed sharp in the air when Jerome's lips left her neck. He whispered roughly into her ear. "Like this?"

She felt him retreat slowly from her walls and Tasha's eyes widened as Jerome slammed quickly again into her heated core.

"I can't hear you Tash." Jerome said before lifting her up by her waist and pumping twice in rapid succession. "Tell me how you want it."

If someone had told her a year ago that this is what sex with a preacher's kid was going to be like, she would have cackled in their face. Yet here she was, being worked well into submission by the love of her life. Tasha was never too big on prayer, but she had to remind herself to start thanking the big OG for the blessing that was now her husband.

Lost in her thoughts, Tasha hardly noticed Jerome reaching out to grab her hand. He pulled her close as he leaned back onto the couch, leaving Tasha no choice but to follow. Their thighs slapped against one another as Jerome thrusted in and out of her warmth, causing Tasha's heavy breasts to sway against his chest. "Yeah, like th-this."

Jerome gripped her tighter, dipping his head to taste the sweat that fell between her chest. Tasha's eyes closed as her core tightened from the feel of his hot tongue. Biting her bottom lip to hold back a moan, Tasha lifted her hips and brought them down to meet Jerome's as he pushed upward. Hearing him groan left her even wetter and the sounds of their loving amplified.

"Don't hold back, let it out." Jerome murmured against Tasha's skin. "I wanna hear you."

His low command sparked the beginning of Tasha's sweet hot release. With his hands on her waist, slowly dragging down to her ass, Tasha knew she was about to come. In between Jerome's strokes, he claimed her lips. When he let go, Jerome bit down gently on her bottom lip, eliciting a whine from Tasha as her thighs moved faster. She threw her head back and opened her mouth, letting another cry of ecstasy spill from her lips.

"Yeah, just like that. Rain on me." He growled.

A second later Tasha's heated core gripped Jerome's dick and she froze while Jerome continued to pump steadily in and out of her slippery folds.

"Ah, Ahhhh, I- Rome!" she shouted.

His release soon followed, filling Tasha as he held her tight before bringing his head to hers. Silence fell over the space while Tasha weakly trailed her fingertips along Jerome's chest, stopping just at his collarbone. She stared down and brought her lips to the space in between his collarbone.

As much as Tasha loved making love to Jerome, the moment after was easily her favorite. Having him close, listening to his heartbeat, and knowing that they were truly together felt incredible.

"I could stay like this all day with you." Jerome said softly.

She felt the same, but knew that the folks in their lives would be too through with them for putting their shopping and lunch plans on hold. Tasha took that moment to remind Jerome, "Remember the last time we stayed in all day when we had plans? Eva and Alexa both were ready to come knocking down our door."

The two chuckled and Jerome leaned closer to kiss her cheek. "I remember, and I ain't sorry. We'd only been back from our honeymoon for two days."

*It still feels like we're on our honeymoon...*she thought. *And I hope that feeling never ends.*

Chapter Two
Run in With a Scourge

After showering and having breakfast together, Tasha and Jerome left their home to stop by the Hearing Center. And since he was not on tour, Jerome wanted to stop by and see what donations he could make for the families in need this year. As they stepped out of the SUV, Tasha's phone rang.

"Heya Trish! I ain't forget about our shopping trip today." Tasha said while she watched Jerome come over to her side of the car and opened the door.

She listened to laughter and music playing in the background before her sister spoke again, "Hey - I know it's last minute but can we meet tomorrow? Lloyd's family came through early and they already done turned our place into a house party."

Stepping out of the car, Tasha heard someone shout and cheer as the unmistakable sound of dominoes hit a table. Jerome now stood in front of her, placing his lips in between the space between her neck and shoulder. She tried to back away but he had her in place with his arm. "Sounds like I'mma have to be. I'll call you tomorrow to see when you free."

"I'm sorry." Trisha offered again. "We wasn't expecting them til tomorrow."

Tasha rolled her eyes at Jerome as he looked at her with a smirk. "It's cool, I understand. Just don't let Lloyd lose all y'alls cash today - Love you!"

Trisha giggled before the two ended their call.

"See? We could still be at home." Jerome said, earning himself a swat on the forearm.

She didn't want to tell him that she agreed, so instead reminded him about the rest of their day. "You still need to go shopping for Ro. Then we're meeting Mama Evelyn for lunch, so stop playing."

The mention of his namesake sobered Jerome up and she wished for a second that she didn't say Ro's name. Tasha knew that this year would be difficult for Jerome, as it was the first one since Ro was born that Jerome wouldn't be with him. She already felt partially responsible, no matter how many times he told her otherwise.

Tasha even offered to spend the holidays with her best friends Alexa and Rachel when he told her the news, but the hardened glare that flashed on Jerome's face on that day told Tasha just what he thought about that idea before he said a word. *"We are not spending our first holiday as husband and wife apart, Tasha."*

A quick kiss on her cheek from Jerome brought her back to the present and she returned his affections with one kiss of her own.

"Okay. Let me go inside and speak to the manager right quick then" Jerome said before adding, "Are you sure you don't want to come shopping with me?"

If Sophie saw her while Jerome stopped by, Tasha could only imagine how tense that would make their new co-parenting arrangement. *Sophie needs more time.* So as much as she wanted to, Tasha shook her head no. Jerome locked eyes with her and neither of them spoke. Dropping his shoulders, Jerome kissed her again before going inside.

Looking at her phone, Tasha scrolled down to her contacts. Calling 'wifey #2', she grinned as Rachel's voice came over the line. "Well ho ho ho sis! How you doing?"

"Alright! Just wanted to say hey and see if we're all still on for our Friendsmas when you and Alexa get back in town."

Hearing giggling in the background, Tasha waited for Rachel to speak again. "Yeah, our place is still a go for then."

"Okay. Tell Alexa I said hey. Love y'all!"

She could hear her best friend and 'wifey #1" in the background, "Love you too!"

Rachel laughed as she ended the call, not bothering to say bye.

I guess tis the season for folks to get it in. Tasha thought with a grin.

Turning to face the center, she let out a deep sigh at the sight of the last person she wanted to see.

. . ∽ . .

PATRICK COULDN'T BELIEVE this mess.

Now that daddy retired from the force, mama had been talking real loud about him finally getting a job. At first he thought she was joking until he received an application instead of her normal home cooked breakfast that morning.

"What's this? Where's my plate?" Patrick huffed out, holding the paper in his hand like it was a dirty pair of draws.

Mama sat down at the table and produced a pen. "Mobile Titan is hiring. Fill out that paper and take it to their office - today." She then pushed the pen toward Patrick.

"Man! You serious right now?!" he shouted. "Is this about my trip last month? I said I was sorry!"

I know I was wildin' hard in Atlanta with the boys but this shit's too much!

He looked up at her and saw mama's face had remained unchanged. "Your daddy and I agree that it's time for you to earn your own money Patrick. We're ready to enjoy our retirement, so you need to start taking care of yourself."

Patrick's mouth dropped out as she walked away, leaving him without anything to eat.

Leaving his house, Patrick stopped at Wayward Waffles and bought his breakfast with the money he took from daddy's wallet that morning. While waiting on his to-go order, he asked the cashier if they were hiring and when they looked back at him and laughed, Patrick wanted to slap the black off their ass. *All you had to do was say no, withcho burnt chicken nugget looking ass.*

While he waited on his food, Patrick took out the crumbled application from his back pocket and used the pen that was left on the counter to fill it out. A few minutes passed before his food arrived and he grabbed it, taking the pen with him before leaving for Mobile Titan.

Parking his ride, he went inside and walked up to the girl at the counter. "Y'all hiring?"

The receptionist at the counter looked around the office before speaking. "Yes. Would you like an application?"

"Nah, I'm good." Slapping the crumbled paper onto the counter, Patrick smiled.

Scanning the application, the receptionist sighed. "I see, thank you Patrick Caine. Once your application is on file with us, we'll also need you to submit a drug test. When will you be available to schedule a date and time for testing?"

Patrick's mouth dropped open. Cutting his eyes at the receptionist, he snatched up the application. "Nevermind."

Marching out of the office, his brows were twisted together as he thought over what just occurred. *What they need a damn drug test for? Trying to steal my DNA and shit!*

Pacing the sidewalk, Patrick looked up and sees Tasha and Jerome. Grinding his teeth, he watched Jerome kiss Tasha and he spits on the concrete. *I heard they had their little wedding a minute ago, guess they got tired of being on the low.*

He continued to eye Tasha as Jerome went inside one of the buildings nearby, while she talked on her phone. Licking his lips, Patrick zeroed in on her full chest and smirked as he lowered his gaze down to Tasha's hips and ass. *She still heavy, but I could work around that to get to the pudding. It must be good as hell to get the preacher's kid to wife her ass.*

• • ⌘ • •

WISHING SHE'D STAYED in the car, Tasha narrowed her eyes on Patrick. She chose to ignore him and started to make her way back to the parking lot. "Happy holidays." he sneered.

Tasha gritted her teeth at the smirk on his face and willed herself to keep walking away. *Just ignore his punchable face for a few more feet and you good.*

"You uppity ass still too good to speak?"

As she made it past him, Tasha breathed a sigh of relief, until he scoffed. "Looks like PK done split you wide open. I know your ass wasn't always that fat."

She froze to the spot, her anger rushing to the surface. *OG, I tried your way and that ain't work.* Twisting both sides of her neck, Tasha balled up her right first and started to turn back around to deck Patrick's halls. Though before she could get a word out, Tasha heard another voice.

"Say another word to my wife and I'll crack your jaw."

It was a sunny afternoon, but Tasha felt a chill as Jerome marched over toward her side. She didn't even see when he stepped out of the hearing center. Looking into his eyes, Tasha knew that Jerome meant what he said and the last thing she wanted was to have to bail her husband out of jail just before Jesus' alleged birthday.

She had seen more than her fair share of dudes pretending to be the big bad in their crew, but the way her husband was looking at Patrick right told her that he wasn't pretending. In fact, the look she saw would for sure give her nightmares nightmares. The cold, steel glare that he sent Patrick's way had her thinking quickly how to get Jerome's attention. She reached out and touched his cheek. Only when Tasha saw Jerome's eyes soften as he met hers did she breathe.

"You'll what PK? Just cause you bought the cow..."

Jerome started to take steps toward Patrick and Tasha rounded in front of him. Using her hands, she spoke as fast as her limited ASL would let her, "He not worth it. Please, let's go."

She sent a silent prayer that Jerome wouldn't notice the slight tremble as she put her hand on his cheek again. When he closed his eyes, Tasha used that moment to push him two steps backward before turning to face Patrick.

"Happy holidays, asshole."

Grabbing Jerome's hand, Tasha practically sprinted away from the plaza, dragging Jerome along the way.

"Tasha, slow down." Jerome finally said.

She waited until they were a hundred meters away from Patrick before coming to a stop. That was the first time Tasha had heard or seen Jerome in that manner and she didn't want him to see how it made her feel. Looking at him, Tasha forced a half smile to her face. "I thought I was the hothead in this relationship."

"Marriage." he corrected.

Tasha forced out a laugh and Jerome's face remained unchanged. "You know what I mean."

When she tried to let go of his hand, Jerome gripped it even tighter. Her pulse quickened as he stared back at the direction that they'd left. "He ain't gonna have too many more times to speak to you out of pocket Tash, know that."

Oh, if she didn't know then, Tasha sure as hell knew it now. And it set her teeth on edge to think of what Jerome was ready to do to Patrick. Trying again, she spoke, "Rome, please let it go. We been knew how Patrick is and -"

Jerome cut her off. "No. I ain't letting it go again! The way he was looking at you...and what he said..." His chest rose and fell before he tightly shut his eyes. "You are my *wife* Tasha. And I don't care how I have to teach Patrick that - he *will* show respect to our union."

His free hand curled into a fist, and Tasha could only imagine just how Jerome would 'teach' Patrick to put some respect on their marriage. She reached out and took his fist into both of her hands. Raising it, Tasha pressed Jerome's fist gently across her lips. When

Jerome's eyes followed her movements, she spoke softly. "You're right, I'm your wife. And as your wife, let me remind you of two key things."

Tasha lowered their joined hands to her chest. "Nothing that fool says will ever change or challenge the marriage vows we made to each other. And..." Surveying the plaza to make sure no one was within earshot of them, Tasha continued, "I can think of far better uses of these hands."

Jerome chuckled as Tasha kissed his fist again. Releasing it, she sighed as Jerome unclenched his hand and placed it across her cheek. "You can, uh?" he teasingly asked.

Tasha nodded.

"Okay. I'll try to keep that in mind."

"You better. Now let's go and see Mama Evelyn."

Chapter Three
These are Special Times

The Seafood Shack was busy and Tasha was glad that Mama Evelyn arrived earlier and got them a table outside. "My babies! Y'all finally made it!"

She grinned as Evelyn stood and opened her arms. The two held each other close for a while until Jerome finally spoke, "Sorry we were running late."

"Boy hush, I know y'all still newlyweds." Evelyn told him before adding with a wink, "Just glad to see y'all letting each other up for air these days."

Tasha fought the blush that started to creep into her cheeks while Jerome cleared his throat.

"Now, I'm just teasing. Sit down so we can finally eat - I'm starving!"

Soon the trio ordered and while waiting on their meals to arrive, Tasha couldn't help but notice Evelyn staring at her. It felt different somehow, but she dismissed the thought. *You probably still feeling off after dealing with Patrick dumb ass.*

Choosing to focus back on the conversation, she listened as Jerome told her about their plans to donate toys and grocery store gift cards to the families in need at the hearing center. "We thought it would be better if we did it anonymously, so we wouldn't have to deal with the press."

"That's good baby. I love that y'all are giving back this season." Evelyn said.

Jerome took Tasha's hand into his, "Me too."

Kissing the inside of her palm, Tasha closed her eyes and as she opened them again, Evelyn was staring directly at her. Their food also arrived and things went silent as Jerome blessed their meal, not bothering to let go of Tasha's hand.

Eating their fill of fried fish, hushpuppies, and boiled corn on the cob, the three slowly sipped on their drinks.

"I'll go and pay for our meals." Mama Evelyn said, but Jerome was up out of his seat.

"Mama, stop playing. I got it."

Tasha watched her husband make his way to the cashier to pay for their meal.

"So, how you been feeling lately Tasha?" Evely asked gently.

Looking across the table, Tasha answered, though she wasn't sure where the question was coming from, "I'm doing alright. Trying to enjoy having a few more weeks off from work."

That much was true. Both her and Jerome agreed to not take on any work until after the New Year and Tasha wanted to enjoy as much of their time together as possible.

When her mama in law scooted her chair closer toward Tasha's, Evelyn brought her voice to a whisper, "I don't mean to be all in your business, but I couldn't help but notice the changes."

What is she talking about? What changes? Tasha wondered.

Her confusion must have shown, as Evelyn then asked, "Is your cycle still on schedule?"

Tasha heard the question and found herself trying to remember when her last monthly visit was. Evelyn grinned, reminding Tasha of someone who knew a secret. "They say the first one is hardest to tell."

When she realized that she hadn't had her cycle in over a month, Tasha's head snapped back up to meet Evelyn's. "Are you saying that you think - that I am..."

"It's been some time since I've experienced it myself, but baby girl, I think so."

Blinking her eyes to stop the tears that begin to surface, Tasha's heart soared. Her and Jerome talked about growing their family since going public with their engagement, and just the possibility of that starting now left her speechless. *I know that's what we want, but could it really be happening?*

Evelyn reached across the table and grabbed ahold of Tasha's hands. The two held unshed tears in their eyes through their smiles until they heard Jerome return. He looked between the two of them and laughed. "I see y'all couldn't wait for me to leave to gossip uh?"

Too afraid of her emotions, all Tasha could do was keep her eyes on Evelyn, who helped her up from the table. "Boy hush! We was just checking in with one another." She squeezed Tasha's hand. "Ain't that right Tasha?"

Hearing her name, Tasha nodded and the three walked out of the restaurant.

When they were in front of Evelyn's car, the older woman pulled Tasha into another tight hug before getting in her car and putting on her seat belt.

"We'll see you next week mama, okay?" Jerome said.

"Alright baby. I can't wait to hear from y'all." Evelyn said, keeping her eyes on Tasha.

Only one thought played in Tasha's mind as they went back to their car, *I need to know if I'm pregnant - now.*

"Can we stop at the pharmacy right quick?" she said to Jerome while staring straight ahead at the road.

"Why? You okay?"

Tasha finally turned to face Jerome. His deep warm eyes were on hers while they waited for the light to change, and she had to remind herself to breathe. *I need to know - now.*

"I just want to pick up a few things before the weekend." she said.

Keeping her voice even was getting harder to do, and Tasha almost said a prayer of thanks when Jerome didn't ask her any more questions. With her uncertainty clawing at the corners of her mind, Tasha said nothing as Jerome walked inside the store with her.

"So, what was it that you wanted?" Jerome asked again.

Tasha was too scared to speak, so she wordlessly led them to the contraceptive aisle. Meeting his eyes, she saw them widened and went back to looking at what she came for. The rows of pregnancy tests surrounding them almost became a blur, until Tasha picked up the one closest to her. *I haven't taken one before...what if I mess it up?*

That thought prompted her to pick up another test. *I heard that some of these can give false positives...I should buy extras, just in case..right?* She wondered.

Feeling Jerome's eyes on hers, the two quietly went to the check out register to pay for the five pregnancy tests that she placed on the counter. The cashier looked at them and the tests before jokingly asking, "You think you got enough tests?"

"It's my - our first time taking one." Tasha said quickly.

Jerome placed Tasha's hand into his and handed the cashier his credit card.

Neither of them spoke again until they opened the door to their house and Tasha kicked off her shoes.

"Do you think - could you be pregnant?" Jerome blurted out.

She stared at him and almost laughed out loud, "The way we've been at it Rome?! Are you seriously asking me that right now?"

Jerome's smirk was on full display, as he rubbed the back of his head while looking down at the bag in his hand.

"I'm late, so I thought maybe I should check. You know, to see if I need to see a doctor to confirm."

Nodding quickly, Jerome held out the bag of tests. "Can you take a test now? How long do we have to wait?"

Reaching inside the bag, he pulled out one of the tests and scanned the instructions while walking toward their bedroom. "Okay, so it says after taking the test we'll know in - "

"Rome."

Midway to their bathroom, he whipped around.

"You planning on taking the test?" Tasha teasingly asked.

She stared down at the bag still in Jerome's hand and waited for his eyes to follow.

"Um, oh!" Jerome handed Tasha the test kit in his hand and Tasha tried not to grin as she walked past him to go inside.

Okay, here we go.

. . ⁓ . .

HEARING THE WATER FROM the sink running, Jerome stared at the open bathroom door and waited for Tasha to come out. When she did, he willed himself to wait for her to say something. She looked at her phone and pressed a few buttons before looking back at him, "Now we wait for two minutes."

"Two minutes. That's it?" Jerome said.

Tasha nodded and he finally went to her, pulling Tasha into a hug. She rested her head on his shoulder and Jerome steadied his breathing. "How do you feel?" he asked gently.

"Right now?"

Jerome waited for Tasha to say more, rubbing small circles on the small of her back to keep his hands busy.

"I feel...scared. Good, but excited. Does that make sense?"

Tasha looked up at him, and Jerome immediately brought his lips to her forehead. He thought of what he wanted to say as he released his hold and Tasha took hold of her hands. "I think so. I feel almost the same way."

"Oh." was all Tasha managed to get out, so Jerome decided to let his heart lead the conversation.

"When I saw you pick up that first test, I was scared. Then I remembered that this is exactly what I saw for us - what I asked The Lord to give us."

Tasha looked at him and whispered, "But what if I'm not pregnant? Will you be -"

Jerome lips met hers and he tried to seal away her worries with the connection before pulling away. *Is that what has you so quiet?* He thought to himself.

"Whether you are or not, we will be okay. We are okay Tash, please know that."

She nodded "I know. I just...I really want to start a family with you."

Searching her eyes and seeing the love and hope that lay behind her irises, Jerome brought their joined hands up to his lips.

As she stared at him, Tasha spoke softly, "Can you - can we just, um...pray right quick? Before seeing what the test says?"

His heart grew in size after hearing Tasha's request. They both lowered their heads and Jerome's throat burned as he spoke with conviction filling his voice, "Dear Father, please continue to keep us in good health. Not only in mind and body, but spirit. As we uplift and praise you, Lord, know that we will never waver in our trust in you."

Pausing to calm the thudding of his heart with a deep breath, Jerome continued. "We ask that you continue to look over our family - whether it remains as it is now, or changes in the future, we thank you Lord for all your blessings. And I pray - I pray Heavenly Father that you continue to aid me in providing love and protection for the healer that you have entrusted with my heart. In your name we pray, Amen."

Opening his eyes to see Tasha staring at him with unshed tears, she whispered, "Amen."

He let go of Tasha's hand and reached out to gently caress her check. Jerome opened his mouth to say more, but Tasha's phone began to ring. The two of them slowly stood up and went into the bathroom together.

As Tasha picked up the test, Jerome's heart was at ease. Now that he knew whether or not their family would be growing more this year or the next, the two of them would enjoy as many moments as possible - together as husband and wife.

No matter what the holidays had in store for them in the future.

This sweet and heartwarming romance read features Jerome Grant and Tasha Daye-Grant, the leading characters found in K. McCoy's debut novel, **A Dove's Cry.**

You can now read their love story from the very beginning by visiting K. McCoy's website, www.authorkmccoy.com[1]. While there, be sure to join her newsletter The Stories Stations for more sweet updates on the continuation of their story, **Doves Cry Too!**

And since 'tis the season of spreading holiday cheer, please enjoy this four chapter excerpt to the sequel of Tasha and Jerome's love story, **Doves Cry Too**!

Doves Cry Too (Excerpt)

By K. McCoy

Finding Peace
Jerome

After finishing up his latest tour, Jerome was glad to wind down for the next six months. Sending a head nod to the bodyguard on duty as he passed through the metal detectors inside *Bottom's Up*, Jerome made his way to the VIP section in the back of the gentlemen's club. His crew wasted no time grabbing girls from the floor to entertain them while they waited for the bottle service to get to their table.

"Your usual, JPK?" a petite hostess asked sweetly, batting her eyes in his direction. Jerome nodded as he settled into the soft leather seat. "Be right back." She purred, swaying in time to the beat of the music as she made her way toward the main bar.

Each of the guys now had two girls sitting on their laps. The girls' delicate hands could be seen even under the dim light, grazing across each other's skin, stopping ever so slightly at their hips and breasts. One girl in particular, with a tawny complexion and shiny red lips, brought her arms closer together when she was touched by her lap mate, a bronzed beauty whose jet black hair spilled down to her backside. This made the tawny girl's already large chest burst through the thin straps of her floss, giving the entourage even more of a show.

Jerome continued to watch as the dancers in their VIP section giggled while rolling their hips and sinking further into the front of the guys' midsections. Any other time he would have looked away, but tonight he found himself almost welcoming the distraction. It was better than the thoughts he had about the latest tracks he received from the new producers that the record label paired him with for his next album. Considering that Jerome hadn't released any new music in over a year, he was in no position to put up a fight.

The beats are good, but I ain't feeling them.

The VIP hostess had returned with his drink, a double whiskey with a cola, cold and still in the can. He handed her a fifty-dollar bill, and the woman winked as she sat his drink down. His soda sat unopened as Jerome picked up the glass of whiskey and took two quick sips.

He looked out into the crowd and watched the men surround the closest stage, tossing bills onto the floor in front of the nearly naked women dancing in front of them. Jerome released a heavy sigh as he sank deeper into his seat before shutting his eyes.

None of this is for me. Lord, what am I supposed to do?

• • ᴥ • •

TASHA

Hearing the news about the woman who birthed her being dead was one thing, but as Tasha stared down at the simple tombstone, her heart was a drift.

She stared at the engraving, which was basic to say the least in comparison to the more elaborate and grand tombstones that surrounded it. For a second, Tasha briefly wondered why her little sister chose to add the simple sentence following Kitty's name at all.

Tabitha 'Kitty' Daye
Beloved daughter and mother.

It'd been four years since she'd been home, and longer than that since she had a kind word to say about her mother. Maybe that was why Tasha's mind still needed a tangible confirmation of Kitty being six feet underground. It was something she had wanted to see for well over a decade, and only having Trisha's word and her eyes to serve as confirmation of Kitty's departure was not enough. Taking out her film camera, Tasha kneeled in front of the tombstone until she was at the level of contrast she wanted. Holding her breath, her hands remained steady, even as her eyes wavered before snapping the picture.

I hope her soul is at peace. That's more than I thought I would ever hope for her.

To calm her rapidly beating heart, Tasha decided to take a walk around the cemetery. With it being the middle of the day, only a handful of people could be seen sitting or making their loved ones' tombstones prettier with flowers and balloons around the quiet grounds. Several large clouds shielded her from the bright sun, which encouraged her to stay longer. Soon she was back in front of the gravesite entrance, just as a steady gust of wind swirled around and added to the sting around her eyes. She allowed herself one last glance behind her to where Kitty's final resting place was and clenched her jaw.

Her feet stomped along the patches of grass and dirt road gravel as she went to her motorcycle. Since she only came to town to see the tombstone in person, Tasha decided not to get a standard rental. Now that she had done what she had come to do, she longed to hop on the bike and sail out of town as fast as she could.

Turning the key into the ignition, Tasha's thoughts went from seeing Kitty's final resting place to her therapists' advice on how to begin forgiving her mother for what her illness cost them.

Having to say goodbye to someone you never really got to know was a strange thing. But in order to find peace for the little girl in her heart to heal, Tasha was willing to try.

I need more time.

Hearing a familiar voice, one Tasha didn't think she'd get to hear again, she turned around. A little boy could be seen running her way, and Tasha's heart leaped into her throat. "Devin?"

He nodded excitedly as she squatted down to look at him closer. He was the spitting image of Trisha. Devin asked with wide eyes. "Titi, why you wasn't at the goodbye thing for granny?"

Before she could answer, Tasha noticed Trisha, with a very swollen belly, and her youngest nephew, Darnell, wobbling toward them.

"I told you to wait, De-" Her sister stopped and stared as Tasha stood back up. "It really is you." Trisha said while rubbing her lower belly.

"Darnell, this Titi. 'member?"

Darnell tilted his head as he looked up at Tasha before walking behind his mama.

He doesn't recognize me. I've been gone that long?

"TiTi, can you come to my school next next Friday?"

Completely caught by surprise, Tasha managed to ask, "W-why do you want me at your school D?"

The boy beamed, hearing her call him by his nickname.

"It's professions week! All the other kids have their mama's and daddy's coming to talk about their jobs, but mama ain't working so she can't come."

Tasha stared at her sister's stomach and offered a weak smile.

"Well, she needs to rest, D." Tasha walked over to Devin and patted the top of his head.

"You ain't gotta come, Tash." Trisha finally said, as someone called out to them.

Tasha watched as a guy, about six feet tall and with bleached blonde hair in a set of cornrows, marched over to join them.

"Didn't we tell ya to wait for us?! Why that boy just up and leave like that?" he barked.

Tasha watched as Trisha looked between the man and Devin.

"Baby, he ain't mean to. Just - he saw his auntie and wanted to say hi, is all." Trisha explained.

The guy frowned down at Tasha and she didn't like him on site.

As he slowly glanced at her from top to bottom, he drawled out, "Well, shiiit, my bad. I thought Tina was your only sister." Tasha willed her stank face away as Devin stood closer to her. "You ain't gonna speak, sista-in-law?"

Tasha's eyes narrowed. "I'm not a dog."

Turning back to Trisha, she asked, "What is he talking about? Sister-in-law?"

Trisha giggled as she waved her left hand in Tasha's face. "I'm finally married! Lloyd, this my sister Tasha, Tasha, this my husband, Lloyd Wrice."

At hearing that news, Tasha took a step back as she looked between Trisha and the man now looming over her.

"Congrats." was all Tasha could manage to say before she kneeled down to talk with Devin again. "What school you go to now, D?"

"Woods Edge Elementary," he told her.

Tasha smiled as she cupped his cheek. "Okay, I'll call the school and sign up for your event, okay?"

He flashed her a big grin and nodded. "Okay Titi!"

Not sure if Devin was still a hugger like when he was younger, Tasha made a fist with her right hand and held it out in front of him. When the little boy did the same with his hand, the two leaned in and tapped their knuckles together. Tasha looked up at her sister and Lloyd. He was standing close to Trisha, whipping his head back and forth between them. It had been years since Tasha had to endure anyone doing a blatant double take when it came to her or one of her more 'presentable' sisters. With their tan brown complexions, light brown eyes, and slim thick figures being the exact opposite of hers, many folks didn't believe they were really related until they learned her last name.

"Why wasn't you at the funeral?" Lloyd questioned.

Tasha's stank face was now on full display as she ignored him and turned to face Trisha.

"Tina thought you wouldn't come, but I still thought you should know, you know?" Trisha said.

Tasha offered her little sister a smile. "Thank you. I just left her gravesite."

She saw her sister's eyes get a little glassy and decided it was time to go.

"Well, I have to go check into my hotel, so... take care, Trish." Tasha said gently.

Her sister held her stare for a beat before she wobbled over and wrapped Tasha in a hug.

Trish sniffled and laughed. "These babies got me all emotional these days."

Tasha blinked several times. "Babies?"

"Yeah girl, twins this time."

Tasha grinned. "I'm happy for you."

She truly was happy for her baby sister. All Trisha wanted was a big family to love and care for, Tasha knew that. She just hoped her gut was wrong about her new husband.

· · ⚓ · ·

"TERROR! GET DOWN!"

Tasha tried not to laugh at the sight of Alexa stepping over the doggie gate to open the door to let her in. She took off her helmet and shook her twists loose, enjoying the feel of them swaying softly near her backside as the tiny French bulldog's barks echoed from inside the house.

While Tasha was away, Rachel and Alexa bought a new home, just on the outskirts of town. The two-story house was one of the few on the new street, and from the sense of quiet that Tasha felt after riding to their place, she understood why the lovebirds chose to live so far away.

Seeing Alexa open the door, Tasha grinned as she strolled closer to her friend and hugged her. "It is so good to see you!"

"You too! Rachel should be home soon, and I ordered us some takeout."

Nodding as Alexa let her go, Tasha looked around at the open layout of the house. She noticed a few of the photos displayed in the foyer area. Seeing Alexa and Rachel in their college days, spending holidays with their families, and dressed to the nines for an event. Tasha couldn't have been happier to see her two friends' journey in life together. Until she spotted a photo in the far back of the stand. It was their last New Year's celebration together, and the image tugged at her heart, causing Tasha to look away.

"How long have you two been living in the boonies?" she asked, as the tiny dog made its way to her feet.

"You got jokes." Alexa said before answering Tasha, "Two years. As soon as I got my promotion, we found this place."

Taking off her shoes, Tasha made her way to the living room to sit on the large suede couch. She looked out at the patio area and noticed the bright tea lights that were strung up outside, surrounding a small sitting area and what looked like a fire pit.

"I'm happy for y'all." Tasha told Alexa sincerely.

She hadn't seen them since their surprise visit three years ago, when she was shooting for a new concierge company in Portugal. Although she loved her work, Tasha couldn't help but feel separated from everyone that she knew and loved before going abroad to pursue her dreams of seeing the world as a photographer. Thinking back to her run in with Trisha and the kids, Tasha felt a hollowness begin to grow within her chest. Until the dog jumped onto her lap, wagging their tail in Tasha's face.

"Terror, no!" Alexa shouted as Tasha laughed.

"It's alright." She said, reaching out to scratch behind the puppy's ears.

Alexa joined her on the couch and looked on as Tasha continued doting on the little dog before clearing her throat.

"We heard about your mama. You okay?" Alexa asked softly.

Tasha nodded. "I went to her burial site before coming here."

The two sat in silence until they heard the sound of keys jingling at the door.

"That's my baby." Seeing Alexa's eyes light up as she jumped off the couch to greet Rachel made Tasha smile.

• • ↯ • •

MUFFLED VOICES MINGLED with the sweet sounds of smooches reached Tasha while she stood and took her time walking back toward the foyer area. She didn't get halfway around the large couch before Rachel sprinted toward her, throwing her whole petite self into Tasha's arms.

"Hey Rachel!" Tasha squealed as she lifted the shorter woman into her embrace.

"Aye, I'mma need you to unhand my woman, Tash." Alexa called out.

Teasingly, Tasha bumped her hip into Alexa's before releasing Rachel, making sure to bring her in for another quick hug.

"It's good to see you Tash!"

While swaying back and forth in Rachel's arms, Tasha fought back more tears. *I didn't know I needed this until now. Thank you Lord.*

As Tasha started to let her go, she reached out for Rachel's left hand and quickly gasped, "Well, okay now! Y'all finally going to stop living in sin, uh?"

Alexa and Rachel looked at one another again as they realized Tasha had noticed the vintage platinum ring on Rachel's left hand.

"It's about time." Tasha said, as she smiled at Rachel.

The couple shared a quick glance with one another, and Tasha tried to shake the feeling that they weren't telling her something. *It's not like I'm always forthcoming right away with them. Just enjoy this time with your girls, Tash.*

Taking her hand away, Rachel reached out for Alexa's and made their way to sit on the wide, dark brown couch. When the two sat down, Tasha joined them.

"Umm...yeah. I popped the question a week ago." Alexa tried to explain. "Before we heard about your mama."

Seeing Alexa struggle to say more, Tasha looked on as Rachel rubbed the top of Alexa's hand with her own. "Yeah, um, we wanted to wait until you arrived to tell you in person. But then Trisha reached out and told us the news."

Tasha slightly brought her head back, taking in everything that they were telling her. *Is that what's bothering them? Right now? Why?*

"Is that why y'all invited me over today? To tell me in person?"'

Not wanting to be the reason they feel awkward sharing their good news, Tasha made sure to add extra merriment to her voice as the corners of her lips turned upward again, "Awww! Y'all are too cute!" The confusion at her behavior was written all over their faces, so she tried again, "What? Did y'all have something else on your mind?"

Rachel started to speak, but Alexa cut her off. "Tash, it's us. You ain't gotta front like everything is okay."

Frowning, Tasha asked, "What you mean, Alexa? Why would I put on a front with y'all?"

After a few seconds passed, Alexa scooted closer to Tasha, as Rachel let go of Alexa's hand and took Tasha's in its place before speaking, "You haven't been home in four years, Tash. And to come back after hearing that your mother passed away? No matter how strained y'all's relationship was, that would be hard for anyone to process."

"We worried about you sis, that's all." Alexa added gently.

Thinking back to when she first read Kitty's tombstone and how she couldn't put into words what she was feeling, Tasha's eyes welled up with tears, which she quickly blinked away. "I love y'all for worrying about me, but I am okay. Really."

Tasha then took their enclosed hands into her own before releasing a shaky sigh.

"My relationship with Kitty has been strained since I was a kid. By the time I finally left, to say that we were well past estranged would have been kind."

Alexa leaned in closer to Tasha, resting her head on Tasha's shoulder.

"And I can work through my feelings about her AND still be happy for y'all! So, what else you two want to talk about tonight? How y'all got the smallest dog ever and had the nerve to name it 'Terror'?" Tasha joked.

Rachel rolled her eyes. "His name is Tyrone Banks-Shaw. Alexa only started calling him 'Terror' after he chewed on a pair of her sneakers."

Seeing Alexa pout, Tasha burst into giggles, and Rachel joined her. Though seeing Alexa's pout deepened before she sucked in her teeth and glanced the other way made Tasha throw her head back in laughter.

"Now see, here I was all ready to ask you to be our maid of honor for the wedding in five months, but I don't think I want to anymore."

Tasha stopped laughing as what Alexa said registered in her head. "Wait, what?" She whipped her head between her two friends. "Y'all want me to what?"

Rachel beamed at Alexa as she confirmed. "Yes, we would like you to be our maid of honor for the wedding."

Tasha launched herself at the two of them, wrapping her arm on either side of her and Alexa before pulling back to look at them both. "Oh my God! Seriously? I would be honored!"

New Intel

Tasha

After saying goodbye to Alexa and Rachel for the night, Tasha called up her freelance partner in Spain, Ximena. When her internship in Argentina ended the first year she left the States, Tasha took a six week second photographer assignment in Spain and fell fast in love with the country. It soon became her home away from home. She met Ximena in the Fall of the same year at an expat networking event. There she learned that Ximena was also an up-and-coming photographer, who used her English fluency skills to assist English-speaking foreigners in her home country. Though for the last three years, Ximena now worked almost exclusively with Tasha.

"I'm glad to hear from you, Tasha. A source told me that Pablo Coslado's Gala is set for fourteen weeks from now."

That got her attention.

While in Murica, Spain for a lifestyle magazine assignment, Tasha had a brief exchange with the reserved, yet globally known photographer on a flight. Though they said no more than a few pleasantries to one another as they went to their business class seats that day, something about him captivated her. When she returned from her trip, Tasha reached out to Ximena to schedule a meeting with him. They learned that he preferred to work alone and even his team had trouble getting him to commit to a schedule. Tasha couldn't shake the need to at least try, so she and Ximena put in the work to find out all they could about the private photographer.

With more failed attempts to secure a meeting with Pablo than Tasha cared to count, they were able to establish a strong business relationship with his people. That kept them up to date on his schedule, which included a yearly gala that the photographer held in a different location. This was the first time in over a decade that the event would be held in his home country, and everyone in the industry wanted a ticket.

Now that they had a timeline, Tasha needed to see about getting an invitation to the highly anticipated gala. "Do you think anyone can secure us tickets?"

"You want *me* to go with you to this event? Why?" Ximena questioned.

Hearing her friend's question, Tasha chuckled, "Why not?" When Ximena remained quiet on the line, Tasha used the time to remind Ximena of just how instrumental she had been in her getting to someday work alongside Pablo Costado. "You have put in as much work as I have to get in the same room as this man - no way I'm leaving you out of the party."

Tasha could hear the excitement in Ximena's voice, "Oh Tasha! That would be incredible! Thank you. "

"Don't thank me yet. I'll get to work on his socials and see if I can find someone who can help us." Tasha told her. "Can you call his team and see if they may be willing to provide us with two tickets, please?"

"Of course Tash!"

Hearing the joyfulness in Ximena's voice when she used her nickname made Tasha fight the corners of her lips from turning upward. Before ending the call, Ximena asked, "So, when will you be returning? Do you have work elsewhere?"

Tasha took out the key to her bike as she looked back at Alexa and Rachel's house. "I just lined up two personal projects. First one is in two weeks, and the next one is a wedding that'll be taking place in four months, which would be right before the gala."

"A wedding? That's quite the surprise. I assume that you still had a preference for not shooting union ceremonies." Ximena stated.

"That's still true, but this happy union is between my two closest friends. And they've asked me to be the Maid of Honor." Tasha explained brightly.

"I see. Congratulations are in order for your friends," Ximena quickly reminded her. "Just please keep me posted, and be sure to rest while away, love!"

Tasha laughed, "You too! I'll be in touch."

. . ⚓ . .

FINALLY MAKING IT TO Creek's Cove Hotel, Tasha settled into her suite and logged onto her computer.

She managed to make it on time for her last appointment of the night, and it was one that she definitely needed after today.

"Hello Tasha."

Looking at the woman who smiled softly back at her on the screen, Tasha offered a small smile of her own. "Good morning, Doctor Richardson."

The woman laughed, "Doctor? You haven't addressed me that way since our first session together a year ago. Is everything alright?"

Tasha stared at the screen as she let the weight of her feelings come forward. "I think so. Just hoping you can help me make sense of why I feel the way I do."

"Well, let's start at the beginning. How are you feeling?"

This was always the hardest part for Tasha when it came to her therapy sessions. She'd learned to keep her feelings to herself. Either to avoid Kitty's hands when she was coming down from a high, or from adults at school who made her feel uneasy whenever they asked about how things were for her at home. It was just safer for her to not tell anyone what was going on in her mind. But now that she was grown, and had found a few people in her life that she felt okay with sharing some things about herself with, Tasha wanted to really explore her thoughts in a safe space. That's when she started looking for a therapist online, and a month later, she found one.

She slouched in her chair and stared at the corner of her screen before answering. "I feel a lot of things. But really, I feel lost. Is that even possible?"

Her therapist scribbled down notes on a notepad and then met her stare. "Yeah, it is. Remember what we talked about Tasha, all feelings are valid, even those that you think aren't possible."

"Right, yeah." Tasha tried to lift the corners of her lips up, but the stinging sensation from earlier returned with a vengeance. She hated crying, especially when talking about something like her feelings. Dabbing her eyes with the helm of her shirt, Tasha went on, "So, my sister Trisha was telling the truth. Kitty died."

"I'm sorry for your loss."

"That's just it. I don't feel a loss. At least not for her." Tasha explained, "I feel bad for my nephews, they really loved their granny. And I'm glad that Trisha wasn't lying just to get money from me."

"You still worry that your sister only reaches out when in financial trouble?" Dr. Richardson asked gently.

"Well, after what happened with Tina, can you blame me?" Tasha snapped.

A few seconds passed before Tasha cleared her throat and spoke again. "Sorry. I just can't help but doubt that either of them want to talk to me about anything else. And Tina still hasn't apologized for what she and Kitty did."

"Do you want an apology from her? Your older sister?"

Picking at the helm of her shirt, Tasha thought the question over. "It would be nice, but so much time has passed... And I'm never gonna get one from Kitty, with her up and gone now."

"You haven't answered the question, Tasha. Is an apology from your sister something you want?"

"I don't know what I want. Which is part of the problem, I guess."

"What do you mean?"

Tasha rolled her neck and took a big inhale. "Well, after seeing Kitty's tombstone, I met Trisha's husband. Then she tells me that she's having twins–how could she tell me about Kitty, but not that she got married? And speaking of getting married, my two closest friends told me tonight that they're finally jumping the broom!"

"You learned all this in one day? That is definitely a lot to take in."

"Right?! Like, yeah, I left home, but seriously! No one thought to call and tell me anything?" The more Tasha thought about the news she got today, the hotter her face felt. "When someone needs my help or my money, they know how the phone works, but when there's good news, I'm the last on their need to know list?"

"It can feel that way, to you."

Sitting up straight, Tasha sent a side eye glance to her therapist. "What's that supposed to mean?"

"Have you ever reached out to your loved ones when things are going well in your life? Just to say hi, or ask about their day?"

Tasha stared at the screen as her left foot bounced against her right leg. She honestly couldn't remember the last time she'd reached out to just randomly call anyone, much less her little sister. "I... I don't - no. I haven't done that." She admitted. "I just figured Trisha was busy with the boys."

She tried not to let her therapist's rapidly moving hand bother her as the woman jotted down more notes.

"It can be difficult at first, but I want you to try to be the one to initiate contact." Dr. Richardson instructed. "Start small, with a simple call to say hello. And see what happens."

"Okay, I'll try." Tasha mumbled.

"So, you received news that your mother passed, your sister is expecting twins with a new husband, and your best friends are finally getting married. Anything else?"

"No, that's about it."

"You said you felt a lot of things, mainly lost."

When Tasha looked down at the keyboards, her therapist continued, "There is another feeling associated with how you're feeling now. And it is common to feel when one is away from their family and friends for long periods of time. You see that their lives are going on, and you are happy for them. But a part of you feels left behind."

"Well, I wouldn't say I feel left behind. Maybe left out of things." Tasha tried again. "I am happy for them, really. I just can't help feeling a little, um, out of the loop."

"What you are feeling, Tasha, is a disconnected from those you love. And that's okay." Dr. Richardson quickly wrote down something else on a notepad before sending another small smile to her through the screen. "So to help you reconnect, I have a small exercise that I want you to try sometime this week before our next session."

Remembering the promise she made to herself to really commit and give this therapy journey all she had, Tasha squared her shoulders back. "Okay, doctor. What is it you want me to do?"

"I want you to disconnect. Spend some time away from your work, your planner, and especially your phone." Dr. Richardson explained, "You've just received a lot of heavy news, and when this normally happens, you retreat from those you are interacting with. So, before your mind begins to go into sensory overload, I want you to spend some time alone with only your thoughts."

Tasha narrowed her eyes at the computer screen as she fought the urge to roll her eyes. "Are you really telling me to shut down? Like I'm a laptop or something?" She chuckled as Dr. Richardson continued, "Well, yes. This is a coping mechanism you've developed as a child. When you feel threatened, or in this case, overwhelmed, you tend to distance yourself from others, for fear of losing your cool or being miss understood in a conversation."

Well, she ain't wrong. Still hard to hear though.

"Take that time to be honest about how you feel and journal those thoughts." Dr. Richardson finished.

Taking a deep breath in, Tasha let her eyelids close as she parted her lips and slowly released the air from her lungs.

"I'm glad to see you're still using the breathing techniques from our earlier sessions."

Tasha stared at the screen and seeing her therapist smiling back at her, Tasha sighed, "They've been helpful."

"And so will disconnecting. Just give it some time, Tasha."

"Well, you haven't let me down yet. So I'll give it a try."

. . ⚓ . .

THE NEXT DAY, TASHA went strolling through the new town plaza next to the hotel. She was hungry and the welcoming smell of fried chicken had her walking toward a small mom and pop restaurant out front. Though before she stepped inside, Tasha saw another building next to it that caught her eye. Curious, she walked closer and stared at the rich, red wooden panels that had several large windows attached to them.

Rows of newspapers were used to cover them from the inside, but a few pages were starting to fall down, exposing what looked like empty bookcases and a winding staircase that matched the panels outside. Stepping up to the windows, Tasha brought a hand to her forehead to get a better look.

Nothing was on the grayish concrete walls, but she noticed several large wooden ladders still leaning against the walls in the far back, and half of a large banner that had the word 'Corner' printed on it that lay on the floor. Just as Tasha began to leave, a man made his presence known, "You looking to buy this building, ma'am?"

Tasha turned around toward the voice. He was dressed in a pair of jeans and a light blue collar polo that complimented his deep sandy complexion. Seeing no reason to be rude just yet, Tasha answered him. "Umm, no. It just caught my eye."

The young man stared at Tasha for a minute before grinning. He took a few steps toward her and Tasha quickly took two steps back. Watching his eyes for any sign of his next move, Tasha blinked as the man in front of her laughed.

"You really don't remember me, Ms. Tasha?"

Confused, she began studying the young man in front of her, relaying his last words in her head. *Wait, he called me Ms. Tasha. Only students I tutored called me that.* "Did I tutor you?"

A grin slowly spread across his face before shouting, "It's me, James! Jay Jay - from Christ Corner."

Recognizing the name, Tasha stuttered out. "W-wait, seriously? Little Jay Jay?"

She heard him laugh again, and now a little embarrassed, Tasha joined him. "I see you finally got that growth spurt you prayed for." She teased.

Watching him bow his head a little and rub the back of his neck, Tasha waited for him to speak.

"Yeah, I did. How you doing Ms. Tasha?"

She waved her hand at the young man. "You grown now, call me Tasha."

Jay Jay flashed her another grin and Tasha couldn't help but notice the crescent moon shape his eyes made when his cheeks lifted, showing her all his teeth.

"I'm doing alright." Tasha told him.

Remembering the property behind her, Tasha asked, "So, you the owner of this building?"

Jay Jay shook his head. "Nah, I just work for the real estate company that does."

"How long has it been vacant?"

"Oh, about two years now. I just come out from time to time to make sure the kids haven't tagged it."

While Tasha was observing the abandoned building, Jay Jay reached into his pocket and pulled out a business card. Handing it to Tasha, he spoke. "Well, it seems like you might be thinking of buying, so here is my card."

"Thank you. It was good to see you."

"Good to see you too, Tasha."

• • ❧ • •

AS TASHA WAITED IN line to pay for her pre-made combo meal from The Pub Grocers deli, she noticed an older woman with their salt and pepper hair in an updo standing a few people in front. *Is that who I think it is?*

Not wanting to embarrass herself or disturbed the woman, Tasha quietly took two small steps to the side as she stole a longer glance at the front of the checkout line. The woman wore a plain pair of slightly loose fitting jeans and an old white t-shirt that had the Christ Corner logo in its center along with the words 'First Lady' written in a fancy script on the left sleeve, which confirmed who she thought the woman was. Tasha's lips instantly turned upward as she stepped out of the line and walked to Jerome's mama. "Mrs. Evelyn?" she called out gently.

When Evelyn turned and faced her, Tasha's heart soared at seeing her return with a smile. "Tasha? Is that you, baby?"

Closing the distance between them, she nodded.

"It's so good to see you!" Evelyn exclaimed, reaching out her arms to embrace Tasha. The two held one another for a minute before Evelyn pulled back to get another look at her.

"You look good, baby girl!"

Tasha's cheeks grew warm from the compliment, and she quickly covered her hand with her mouth.

"You look good too, Mrs. Evelyn."

"Oh, chile hush!"

They shared a laugh before silence fell over them. When Evelyn's grip on her hand tightened, Tasha met her stare. "I heard about your mama, baby girl."

She should've known that Evelyn would have known about Kitty's passing, but it didn't stop Tasha from focusing on the ringing chime sounds of the registers around them as she reminded herself to breathe. Glancing down at the floor, Tasha forced herself to look up and wished she was back inside her hotel room. "Thank you. I just hope she's at peace now."

Evelyn then stepped to the side, gently guiding Tasha along with her. "I know you might be busy, but you want to have lunch together sometime?"

"I'm never too busy to have lunch with you." Tasha said. "How about we both get a meal to go now?"

Evelyn reached out to hug Tasha again. "I'd like that."

The weather was gorgeous, clear skies and a steady breeze welcomed Tasha as she brought her motorcycle to a crawl and stopped in a parking space next to Evelyn's four-door car. Hopping off the bike, she took off her helmet and made her way toward Evelyn, who held their lunches in a plastic bag.

"There's a few empty benches under the pavillon. You want to eat there, baby girl?" Evelyn asked.

"Yes ma'am. Eating there is fine with me."

As she sat everything out, Tasha went to the nearby vending machine to get them something to drink. Coming back to two bottled sweet teas, Tasha handed one to Evelyn, and they sat down together as Evelyn blessed their food.

"So, Tasha, how are your sisters doing?"

Tasha put down her fork and answered, "They doing alright. My younger sister is married now, with twins on the way."

Evelyn's eyes widened. "Twins?!"

"Yes ma'am, twins?" Tasha confirmed, letting out a small chuckle.

Evelyn quickly asked, "You thinking of doing the same someday? Settling down and having some babies?"

She should've known that question was going to come up. And it took considerable effort, but Tasha managed to keep her voice light as she answered, "I think my sister is having enough kids for the both of us. Besides, my work keeps me busy."

"That it do, baby girl." Looking over at Evelyn, who seemed to be miles away. Evelyn's face turned downward and Tasha called out gently, "Is everything okay, Mrs. Evelyn?"

Soon she saw unshed tears fill Evelyn's eyes and Tasha quickly spoke, "I'm sorry, I didn't mean to make you cry."

"I'm fine baby, it's just good to see you, is all."

Tasha took a napkin out of the plastic wrapping from her meal and handed it to Evelyn, who chuckled, "I'm sorry to get like this in front of you."

"It's okay."

More tears fell from Evelyn's eyes as the two stared at one another. Seeing the woman who had always been kind to her, who treated her better than Kitty did while alive, tearing up started to tear at Tasha's inside. So much so that she couldn't ignore the gnawing ache in her chest.

"Please, tell me what it is, Mrs. Evelyn." Tasha gently asked.

Evelyn glanced up at her and wiped the corners of her eyes. Sniffling, she finally answered. "I'm just worried about Jerome. I-I ain't seen or heard from him in weeks! And I don't know what he's been doing these days, or the people he's with. It's just too much sometimes... All I can do is pray he is okay."

Clearing her throat, Tasha pushed aside the many questions she had, questions Evelyn clearly didn't have, as she placed what was hopefully a comforting hand on top of Evelyn's. "I'm sorry Mrs. Evelyn." The older woman grabbed ahold of Tasha's hands and she blinked back her own tears. The need to make Evelyn feel better, to give her even a small amount of peace in that moment is what led her to say, "I promise you, before I leave, I'll find out what Jerome has been up to for you, okay?"

The hopefulness that shone back to her from Evelyn's tear stained face was all Tasha needed to fight the small voice in her mind that told her to not make promises she couldn't keep.

I can do this, find him and let Mrs. Evelyn know he's alright. I can do this - for her.

"Thank you, baby girl."

• • ❧ • •

AFTER HAVING LUNCH with Evelyn yesterday, Trisha and the kids were on her mind. Along with thoughts of her last therapy session urging her on, she picked up the phone and scrolled down until she spotted her little sister's name.

Why am I so nervous to call Trish? Has it really been that long since we talked?

After two rings, Tasha sighed in relief to the sound of Trisha's voice.

"Hey Trish! It's Tasha." she said, letting out a nervous chuckle.

"Oh, hey! What's up?"

Hearing Trisha's casual reply helped calm her nerves a little as Tasha paced back and forth inside her hotel room. "I forgot to ask the other day if you had a baby registry?"

"I do, but don't worry about that." Trisha said

Tasha thought that's what she'd say, so she was already prepared with a response. "Now how can I call myself a good auntie if I don't help out a little from time to time?"

The line was silent for a beat until Trisha spoke again. "Oh, okay. I'm sure by now most of my old co-workers ordered most of the things already. The registry is under 'Wrice for Two' at Loveable Ones Baby Shop."

Tasha wrote the information down. "Okay. I'll see what I can get from the list soon."

Hearing the boys in the background, Tasha remembered the second reason she called, "Oh! I was also wondering if you and the boys had plans today? I would love to see y'all again."

Tasha heard a muffled voice in the background, followed by laughter, before Trisha answered. "We ain't got no plans today, since the kids don't have school. Wanna meet up at Sunshine Park?"

A smile started to spread across Tasha's lips as she remembered spending time with Trisha at the same park, back in the day. "Yeah, I can meet y'all there in an hour."

Quickly getting dressed in a pair of acid washed jeans and a purple tank top, Tasha grabbed her messenger bag and helmet as she walked out of her suite.

Take Care

Alexa

Wayward Waffle's was packed, but Alexa spotted Tasha quickly as they walked inside. Waving her over, Tasha grinned at her and Rachel before joining them at the table, putting her helmet on the empty seat.

"So, why did you offer to treat us to breakfast today?" Alexa asked.

"I was in the area yesterday, visiting Trisha and the kids. So I thought I'd see y'all too." Tasha said cheerfully before adding, "Plus, as your maid of honor, I gotta make sure I know the itinerary so I can help y'all jump the broom in style!".

Rachel grinned. "That's what I'm talking about!"

Alexa watched as Rachel pulled out her planner and Tasha took out her phone. "So here are the dates for the outfit fittings and cake tasting with SweeThangs..."

Seeing the two of them syncing their schedules brought a smile to Alexa's face. And as much as she wanted to believe that Tasha inviting them out for breakfast was only about their upcoming nuptials, Alexa couldn't shake the feeling that there was more to it.

Time will tell soon enough.

Minutes later, a server came by to take their orders and Tasha waited for them to leave before asking Rachel, "How's work been? You like officially running things?"

Alexa looked over at Rachel as she and Tasha started talking about her new position at work. "Yeah! I finally feel like my job is worthwhile again. And being able to pay off my student loans faster with that raise don't hurt none either."

They were all smiles when their server returned with their drinks.

Maybe this really was just a surprise social visit.

Twenty minutes flew by, as the trio chatted about all the things that had changed since Tasha was last home. Everything was going pretty good, until her fiancé gasped, "That's right! You missed the last Jamboree! It was pretty good, even though Jerome -"

Rachel cut her eyes over to Alexis and picked up her drink, taking two deep swigs.

Dang. She would drop his name just when the vibe was so chill.

Tasha seemed unfazed by hearing the preacher's kid's name. She looked at the two of them and sighed. "Y'all can talk about him around me. The man does still live here."

Rachel looked over at Alexa as Tasha continued, "Besides, I already met with his mama the other day. It was... a little awkward at first, but good."

Tasha back in the day wouldn't have told us that. Maybe she really is cool with everything.

"You might be good and all now, but PK ain't." Rachel said. "He's changed over the years and it ain't for the best."

This woman here! Ain't she the one that told me not to say nothing before we got here?

Both Alexa and Tasha look at Rachel incredulously.

"What? I said what I said!"

Watching her fiancé double down on her thoughts about Jerome didn't surprise Alexa. Ever since she reached out to him three years ago on behalf of her company to ask him about possibly mentoring the kids at her center as part of a workshop event, and he all but ignored her, choosing to mail out some autographed CDs and t-shirts instead of calling Creative Chords back. Alexa knew when Rachel tossed the fan mail into the trash that her baby was too through with Jerome 'JPK' Grant.

"Whoa, okay. He must really be something for you to be so vocal about it."

Before Rachel could go in anymore about Jerome's antics over the years, Alexa took out her phone and logged into her social media feed.

She handed the phone to Tasha. "I guess you don't follow him online, uh?" she said as Tasha looked at the phone's screen.

She studied Tasha's face as her friend scrolled down the social feed. When she saw Tasha's free hand curl up slightly, Alexa slowly brought her eyes to the ground. Sure enough, Tasha's left foot was bouncing like a hot rabbit's tail.

Gotta give it to you, Tasha, you almost had me fooled.

"They're just behind-the-scenes pictures of him on stage while touring." Tasha tried to joke, but Alexa wasn't having it.

"He was quiet at first, the year that you left." Alexa looked on as Rachel explained. "Then he started touring more and got real bougie on his socials."

"Rachel, I hear you. But what has he done that is so bad? He looks like every other rapper online these days."

"That's just it Tash. He ain't supposed to be like every other rapper!" Alexa hissed. "He said he's rapping about God to reach the kids, but how that gonna work? With him saying one thing on stage and then going out and partying like the other rappers at Trap Sons?"

The trio got quiet as their server brought out their food. Though the longer she stared at Tasha, who grinned like a little kid as the server placed her plate in front of her, the hotter Alexa's face grew. They watched on as Tasha cut into her fried chicken and waffles, closing her eyes when she brought the food to her opened mouth.

"Dang Tash - you wanna be alone?" Rachel snidely asked.

Rolling her eyes at her fiance, Alexa looked on as Tasha took another bite of her meal. "What? It's been a minute since I've had fried chicken." Looking down at her plate and bringing her lips together once more, Tasha added, "I love mixed paella as much as the next girl, but it don't hit the spot like this plate right here."

"Everything okay here?" Their server asked.

Tasha looked up at them and grinned. "We good. Can you bring us the check, please?"

Their server nodded and walked away.

"So that's it? You ain't got nothing to say about your boy?" Alexa asked Tasha directly as she added, "And he's married now - with a son. You still don't wanna say nothing?"

Taking a swig of her orange juice, Tasha answered. "What should I say?"

Alexa watched Tasha as she tilted her head. A small, tight smile appeared on her face before she continued on. "We wished each other well, and it looks like he's doing just that."

Rachel stared at her plate as Alexa glared at Tasha. "No, actually, he isn't. Not really." She said evenly.

Tasha continued eating her food, seemingly done with their current conversation.

"And I'mma need you to stop frontin' about this Tash!" Alexa finally snapped. "One of our associates at the firm is a member at Christ Corner. They say that folks been whispering about Jerome for years now. How he been missing from service for months, and when he does show up, him and his wife don't even sit together. Some of the kids that he's given autographs and take pictures with say he smelled like a skunk!" Alexa harshly whispered, "Now you tell me - is that behavior normal for a Christian rapper?"

"I wouldn't know. I don't work with entertainers." Tasha replied as their server handed her the check.

"You ain't fooling me Tash with this attitude of yours. Back in the day you and Jerome - *Rome* - y'all had something. You mean to tell us that you don't care what he's been up to now that you're back in town?"

Both Alexa and Rachel stared at Tasha. She finally put down her knife and fork before softening her gaze. "Yeah, years ago, Jerome and I were *almost* more than friends. But I chose different and left. He went on with his life, and I sincerely wished him well. The end."

Hearing Alexa scoff, Tasha went on. "From what y'all have told me, he's done that. Jerome is a successful rapper, husband, and father. Even if I did still have feelings, it wouldn't matter. And if I did have worries about him, it's not like I have the man on speed dial. I don't even know how to get in touch with him these days."

"I bet you'd find him at BU. Last I heard, that's where him and his crew like to go these days."

Alexa was going to have a strong talk with her fiancé later about over sharing. Tasha could pretend all she wanted, but Alexa wasn't fooled.

If she cool with seeing Jerome's mama - it's only a matter of time before they see each other. I just hope it doesn't send her running away for another four years.

"I've got no problem with going to Bottom's Up. It's been a minute since I've been there. Too bad y'all sold The Fast Fix. I could've put in a shift, you know, for old time's sake."

Tasha took another sip of her juice before slowly standing up. "I'm gonna go take care of the bill right quick."

Rachel and Alexa watched their friend walk to the front counter, and Alexa sighed.

"You believe her, babe?"

Alexa slowly shook her head. "I want to, but she trying too hard to convince us that she don't care about him anymore."

"She always did keep her feelings to herself, but babe, I'm really worried for her."

Rachel took Alexa's hand and kissed her knuckles gently. She knew her girl was thinking back to the day Tasha came home after being out with Jerome for the weekend. She and Rachel had spent the weekend indoors, watching reality TV and sipping wine on their couch. Both were tipsy and giggling when Tasha entered the house. They didn't even realize anything was wrong as they started to tease Tasha about getting the preacher's kid to 'sin for the weekend' until Tasha dropped her overnight bag and fell to the floor.

Alexa sobered up real quick at seeing her usually together friend bawling and shaking like a leaf in front of them. That night, she and Rachel took turns passing by Tasha's bedroom door, listening to any hint that she was okay. They'd fallen asleep on the couch and were woken up by the smell of bacon and eggs, along with an apology from Tasha. She told them about the internship she was accepted for, completely avoiding any further talk about her time with Jerome.

And just like that, after one night with Jerome, her best friend of over a decade was gone from her life. All because she fell for the preacher's son and got hurt. *I'm not about to let that happen again, not if I can help it.*

"I just don't want her to get hurt again." Alexa spoke softly as Tasha made her way back to the table.

"Me too babe, me too." Rachel whispered, taking Alexa's hand in hers and kissing it gently.

. . ⤳ . .

SOFIE

"That boy is getting so big!"

Hearing mama comment on little Ro for the second time that day, Sofie rolled her eyes. "Ain't that's what he supposed to do? Can't stay a baby forever."

Lillie Ward tsked at her youngest child before going over to pick up her now sleeping grandson. She grinned as she walked down the hall to put him in bed. While her mama was fawning over her son, Sofie took a glance in a nearby mirror and frowned as she looked down at her stomach.

The thin jagged lines that went around her torso were light, only a shade darker than her overall complexion, but she still detested the sight of them.

Those stretch marks won't go away for nothing!

"I wish you paid as much attention to your baby as you did your body." Lillie Ward shook her head as she marched past Sofie. "Where is my son-in-law these days?" she asked.

Sofie honestly didn't care where her husband was, as long as he kept paying the bills. In fact, the less she saw of him, the better. "He'll be home soon. Which reminds me, do you think you can look after Ro for a little bit? My girl Regine just got back from Miami and I wanna see the new ride her man got her."

Lillie Ward sucked her teeth, "Everybody in town knows that that boy ain't her man."

Not in the mood to hear another one of her mama's lectures, Sofie tried being sweet instead. "I'm just trying to be supportive of my friend. Is that bad?"

Lillie cut her eyes at Sofie. "Fine. Go and see about your little friend."

She quickly threw her arms around Lillie, making sure to give her a peck on the cheek as well.

"Thanks mama! I'll be back soon."

The drive out to visit Regine didn't take as long as Sofie thought it would. Pulling her ride into the guest parking area, she gawked around at the manicured hedges and freshly cut grass that expanded up about a mile, leading to a mansion that was at least half the size of a football field. She knew that Buckem signed with the label a month ago, but now she wondered how much of an advance he got for his first album. Besides her car, three others were parked in the driveway as Regine grabbed her hand and squealed.

"Look at us Sofie! Finally a bunch of married ladies!"

Sofie's arched brow raised as she turned to her friend. "Did you and Bentley get married while y'all were in Miami?"

"Nah, girl. He still tripping about that. But he made sure to ice me up real nice while we was away."

Regine's voice was light, but Sofie didn't miss the pout that came after her friend spoke.

I bet he did 'ice' you up.

Sofie snorted as Regine kept talking. "When we got back, the label told him they was throwing him an album release party! They having the party at BU and invited a whole bunch of artists."

Regine smirked as she lightly touched the sparkling necklace around her neck. "They even invited JPK. I saw the guest list this morning."

Sofie kept her smile in place while looking at Regine, but inside she was ready to go off. She made it clear to her husband once he got back from touring that she wanted to be kept in the loop about where he was at all times. That way, they could continue to live their separate lives and not worry about being in each other's way. But if he got an invitation to this release party–she was going–no matter what their living arrangement was like these days.

I'll find out what happened when I get back home.

"He said that with the mixtape doing so good, they want him in the studio recording. That's why he ain't here now."

That suited Sofie just fine. Bentley 'Buckem' Robson was well known in town, but only recently for rapping. Growing up in the projects, he first showed promise as an aspiring writer. He was featured in a few spoken word events too, until his mama up and died from cancer when Bentley was fifthteen years old. Soon after that, he dropped out of school and was in and out of juvie until he caught an assault and armed robbery charge on his seventeenth birthday. The courts tried him as an adult and he did seven of his twenty five year sentence before being released on good behavior.

Sofie wondered exactly what the system deemed as 'good' behavior, because any time she was within two meters of Bentley, she felt uneasy. She knew of dudes who pretended to be the baddest in their crew, but Sofie knew at first glance that Bentley never had to fake it - he was nothing but bad. The further she was from him, the better. Though once her girl saw Bentley gaining attention as a new rapper on the scene, Sofie knew it was only a matter of time before Regine would try to lock him down.

"That's good." Sofie said absently.

Regine jerked her hand even closer toward her. "Good? That's better than good!"

Using her free hand, Sofie unlocked their tangled hands and tried to rub the feeling back into her arm. "You right. The sooner he gets in the studio, the sooner he can start paying all this stuff off."

Regine cut her eyes at Sofie. "Don't be like that, Sofie. Just cause you bagged a lame -"

"At least *my* rapper put a ring on it. You really think Bentley's gonna do the same?"

Seeing the crestfallen look on her friend's face, Sofie softened her tone before speaking again. "I ain't mean to say all that. I'm just trying to look out for you sis, that's all."

Regine rolled her eyes as she bumped hips with Sofie. "Girl, look 'round you! Someone IS looking out for me - I'm in this big ass house, with three whips to choose from when I wanna roll through town! I'mma be alright."

Sofie looked back at the parked cars and sighed.

I should stop being petty. Regine's my girl.

"You right. So, what you got to eat in this big ass house?"

The two laughed as they began walking toward the front door of the house.

· · ∾ · ·

TASHA

After breakfast with her besties, Tasha decided to spend her afternoon editing photos from her last photoshoot in Mexico. Time always did get away from her when she got in the zone of perfecting her photos, and when she looked out the window to her suite, Tasha wasn't surprised at all to see that the sun had set. While submitting the batch of photographs to her client, Tasha's computer rang. She quickly pressed the green receiver button on the screen.

"Hello Ms. Daye. This is Dr. Richardson's office calling. We would like to know when to schedule your next appointment."

Tasha completely forgot to schedule her next therapy session. "Yes, hi. Can I see Dr. Richardson in two days, please?"

Confirming her appointment, Tasha noticed the time and started putting away her things.

Bottom's Up should be in full swing now.

She made her way to the door, grabbing her helmet and keys.

With all the work traffic gone for the day, Tasha was able to pull into the strip club's parking lot within thirty minutes. Like everything else in town, *Bottom's Up* had gone through its own renovations. There were now two separate check points, each with someone from security standing by once patrons stepped inside the building. Tasha paid the entrance fee and waited her turn to be patted down for contraband before being scanned by the metal wand the female security guard held in their hands. One of the guards, a fair skinned, short woman with blondish red hair pulled back into a low ponytail, eyed her a little too long before Tasha finally went through the detectors.

"Empty your pockets," the female guard demanded.

Doing as asked, Tasha eyed her wallet and keys as she went through the detectors again.

Once she was cleared through, Tasha took in more updates of the club. There now were three mini stages, instead of one long stage for the dancers. The only seats available on the floor were directly next to the stages, as the others were elevated up, similar to stands at a colosseum or a football stadium. There were also mini bar stations in opposite corners, giving those walking inside more space to ogle and mingle with the dancers. The lights were still their vibrant neon purple, but glow lights had also been installed, making everyone in white stand out more.

Even the VIP section got an upgrade. Now there was a velvet entrance and two guards that stood in front. Tasha pitied the fool that would try to start something in there, with those menacing gladiators guarding the area. Several hostesses fluttered around in uniformed mesh black dresses. Tasha closed her eyes and tried to re-familiarize herself with the smell of smoke and cheap cologne before she went to talk to the girls. When she opened her eyes, Tasha was greeted by a familiar face.

"Hey Tash. It's been awhile."

Velvet didn't hide her smirk as Tasha took her in. She was only slightly more dressed than the hostesses, yet the nude dress she wore made the woman appear naked when the light hit her just right. Her signature braids were on full display, though now she wore them with beads on the ends. Even over the bass line in the club, Tasha could hear the faint clicking sound they created as Velvet turned to survey the activity around them.

"Velvet. It's good to see you." Tasha finally said.

"The guard out front told me you were here, and I had to see for myself. What brings you by?" she asked.

Knowing that information inside BU came with a price, Tasha made sure to stop by the ATM on her way to the club.

"I'm in town for a few weeks and wanted to swing by. For a friend."

As she removed several bills from her wallet, Velvet grinned. "I always did like that about you, Tash. How you got straight to the point and came prepared."

"One thing I learned from working with y'all is that time is money."

Velvet turned and Tasha followed her to one of the mini bar stations. When she sat down, Tasha joined her and placed two twenties on the counter. Velvet turned her attention to the bartender running the station, and they grabbed a glass and a bottle of what looked like brandy.

"You want anything?" Velvet asked.

"Nah, I'm good, thanks."

Feeling Velvet look her over, the woman tilted her head toward Tasha. "That's right, the other girls used to talk about how you never drink while working. Smart."

The bartender brought Velvet's drink, and Tasha was about to ask how much it was until they said, "Here you go boss."

Tasha waited for them to leave before asking, "Boss?"

Velvet grinned, letting the vivid purple and blue neon lights shine wickedly against her white gold iced out grillz. "For the last two years, I've been managing this place."

"Congratulations." Tasha said as she watched Velvet sip her drink.

"So, what is it that your friend needs from BU, Tash?"

"Just some information, that's all. But it's about a customer. At least I think they may be." Tasha answered as best as she could. "Goes by the stage name 'JPK.'"

Velvet gazed out at the crowd passing by as she took another sip of her drink.

"Who wants to know about JPK?" Velvet asked.

Taking out two more twenties, Tasha placed them with the others. "His mama. She says she ain't seen him in some time, and a friend told me that he might come here."

Velvet nodded, putting her drink down on the counter and eyeing Tasha, who finally had a seat next to her. "He mostly comes in and has some drinks. Buys his boys a few dances in VIP before leaving."

Tasha tried not to let the shock of hearing that Jerome drinks show on her face as she slipped Velvet another twenty.

"Has he been in recently? His mama hasn't seen him in a minute and she's worried." Tasha asked as a new song began to play. Three dancers went to each mini stage at once and they must have been a fave among the horny herd, as all the seats near the dancers quickly filled up. She watched as bills sailed into the air and the girls flirted with the masses, one after the other, taking their turn to show off their pole skills to the cheers of the crowd.

Velvet signaled for the bartender to come over again as she picked up her drink and knocked it back in one gulp. "Yeah, he's been in recently."

Tasha could feel Velvet's eyes on her again and returned her stare as she took out another twenty. "Thanks. It was good to see you again."

She hopped off the stool and surveyed the crowd a bit more.

Just what happened to you Jerome?

Before she could walk back to the entrance, Tasha felt a soft tug on her elbow. Pausing to look at Velvet, the woman casually spoke. "A year ago, we had a girl working here, went by the name Cream. She was the only girl he ever bought a dance for himself from."

Tasha kept her face neutral before tilting her head at Velvet. "I only wanted to know where he is now, not who he got a dance from in the past. But thanks."

Velvet reached into her cleavage and pulled out a small black case. Removing a cigarette, she turned to the bar counter and picked up a pack of matches as she spoke again. "You and Cream favor."

Tasha froze.

"You say his mama looking for him? Why ain't I talking to her instead of you, then?"

Slowly turning to face Velvet, Tasha tried her best to keep her voice neutral. Locking eyes with Velvet, she answered evenly. "His mama's the First Lady at Christ Corner." Sighing, Tasha rolled her shoulders back. "I really don't want to be the one to tell his mama that her only son has been skipping church services to drink at BU. Trust - the minute I find him and give him her message, I'm on the first thing smoking out of here."

Velvet nodded slowly and took a drag of her cigarette. Seeing her completely calm and in her element, Tasha reached into her back pocket.

"I know you run things now, but if you ever want some photos done, I would love to collaborate with you." Tasha said sincerely as she handed Velvet a business card.

She watched Velvet take her card and look it over. The woman then grinned as she slipped the card inside the black case.

"Thanks again for the info."

"You welcome Tash."

These are our Confessions

Tasha

After their last meetup, Tasha and Trisha decided to have lunch with the kids the following week at Roger's Playground, a kid-friendly arcade style restaurant. Tasha arrived before they did and saw Devin and Darnell barreling toward her.

"Hey Titi!"

Bending down to swoop them both in her arms, Tasha listened to their giggles and Trisha tsking.

"Stop picking them up like that girl! You gonna put your back out."

Putting the boys down, Tasha reached into her pocket and took out her wallet. Their eyes lit up as she gave each of them ten dollars. "Y'all can get change inside to play the games. Come back when we call y'all to eat, okay?"

"Okay Titi!"

Tasha laughed as they made a beeline for the change machine.

"You spoiling them, girl." Trisha told her as she sat at the table.

She knew Trisha was right, but Tasha couldn't help it. "I already missed so much time with them. I can't help but be a little extra while I'm here." Tasha explained. "Also, did you get my email? About your registry?"

Trisha squirmed a bit in her seat as she looked at Tasha. "Yeah, I did. Lloyd and I looked at it twice to be sure what we saw was right."

Tasha smiled, "Good. So, how you feeling? What else you need?"

As her baby sister narrowed her eyes at her, Tasha started to brace for a pushback to come. She knew getting everything that was left on Trisha's registry was a bit much, but Tasha remembered when Devin was first born. Trisha worked throughout her pregnancy and still came up short when it came time to get all the things the hospital told her she needed. Hearing her sister cry at night as her newborn slept in the bed beside her, Tasha silently promised that if she could ease Trisha's worries with anything related to taking care of her kid that she would do so without hesitation. And the number of things still left on their registry, with just a few months left, didn't sit right with her, so Tasha bought everything and made sure to schedule it all for delivery by the end of the week.

"It's a lot, Tash, that's all. But thank you." Trisha said. "Lloyd's job has started to cut back on everyone's hours, so things have been a little tight."

"I'm glad I could help, Trish."

And she was. Her little sister seemed to be happy with the family she created, and Tasha couldn't help but be joyful for Trisha.

A server finally showed up and took their order before Tasha spoke again. "I won't be able to see y'all again for a minute. That's the other reason why I wanted to meet y'all today." Tasha continued, "I'll still be here, but Alexa and Rachel are finally tying the knot and asked me to be their maid of honor."

Trisha shook her head as she let out a nervous giggle. "Oh, girl! You had me worried for a minute! All Devin's been talking about is you going to his professional's day at school on Friday."

They shared a laugh as Tasha explained, "That's why I wanted to squeeze in a bit more time with y'all, to let you know that I'm still gonna be at his school."

"That's what's up!"

Tasha looked on behind Trisha, and her eyes narrowed a little. Turning to look in the same direction as her sister, she saw her older sister Tina walking toward them. She wore a pair of form fitting khaki pants and a bright yellow polo shirt that made her fair brown skin pop while showing off her petite frame. With her signature cornrows highlighting her high cheekbones, Tina briefly paused while staring at them.

Tasha hadn't seen her since their fight at Christ Corner four years ago, and it was clear from Tina's dismissive stare that she wasn't here to apologize for helping Kitty steal her scholarship money back in high school. Cutting her eyes over to her baby sister, Tasha watched as she quietly lowered her head.

"Did you invite her?" Tasha asked Trisha directly.

"Not really. I did hope that she had a shift at The Lunch Grill when I messaged her though..."

Tasha rolled her eyes as Tina leaned over the railing of the patio area, completely ignoring her. "Hey Trisha. Where the boys at?"

"They inside on the games until the food gets here."

Tasha looked on as Trisha and Tina shared a glance at one another. She didn't know what it was about, and she didn't care. All of Tasha's instincts told her to get up and leave. But with Doctor Richardson's words about giving people a chance to prove her wrong ringing loudly in her head, Tasha steadied her breathing. *Just try Tash. Not for Tina's sake, but for Trish and the boys. Try.*

"You ain't gonna say hey to Tash?" she heard Trisha say to Tina.

Relaxing her shoulders, Tasha struggled to keep her resting bitch face away as Tina finally looked her way.

"She got eyes too." Tina scoffed before adding, "What, she too good to speak to me?"

"Hey Tina." Tasha mumbled.

When her big sister cackled, it charged up all the horrible memories she had from hearing Tina laugh at her as a kid. Every bone in Tasha's body screamed for her to leave, to be anywhere but here. Tasha glanced behind her and relaxed her jaw at the sight of Devin and Darnell being well out of earshot.

"You don't sound happy to see me, uh biggie smalls?" Tina questioned, pulling out one of her favorite nicknames for Tasha from back in the day. Tasha focused on her breathing as she watched Tina tilted her head before sucking in her teeth. "Food must be real good where you been - you just as big as I remembered."

Trisha frowned. "Really Tina?"

"What? She still can't take a joke? At her BIG age?" Tina countered.

Memories of Tina first picking on Tasha for being fatter than her and Trisha back in the eighth grade came flooding her mind. How the harder she cried from the teasing jabs only made Tina go harder in on her - from her weight to her non relaxed hair - everything about Tasha became one big comedy show. Until Tasha started to use her weight to her advantage and fought back with her fists.

"Forget I bothered." Tasha finally said, "I see you still ain't worth talking to."

Tina rolled her neck before cackling again and looking at Trisha. "See, she don't want to talk to me no way. I guess all that bougie ass traveling ain't changed her for the better."

Tasha turned to face Tina, and Trisha snatched up the silverware near Tasha, causing Tina to laugh.

"Maybe if I had started traveling earlier, like when I was supposed to after high school, I would be more willing to change. Guess that plan, along with yours back then, went up in smoke."

"I see you still think you better than everybody else."

"I see you still broke. By the way, how is that even possible?" Tasha leveled her eyes at Tina and spoke as evenly as possible. "I did the math. You and Kitty had at least twenty thousand dollars transferred to your bank account. You didn't think to save some of the money you stole for a rainy day?"

Tina narrowed her eyes at Tasha before leaning in closer to her face and spitting out, "You always think you got all the sense! If you really was as smart as you act, you would've been knew what happened."

When her hands balled into fists, Tasha heard Trisha harshly whisper, "Y'all, please don't do this here! Tina, just say you sorry so we can all get along again."

Tina whipped her head toward Trisha. "When did we ever get along? Is that why you chose to drag Saint Tasha down here for lunch by my job?"

With both Tina and Tasha glaring at her, Trisha tightly shut her eyes and took a deep breath. "Yeah, okay! With Kitty gone, I thought y'all would be ready to try and make peace with each other." Trisha looked between her two sisters before crying out, "We all we got!"

Tasha looked at Trisha, "Trish, I know you meant well–"

"You don't know shit!" Tina barked out. "When granny died, Kitty would leave me alone at home with y'all for days. I was only 12 years old, alone in a house with no food, sometimes no water or lights, looking after y'all!"

Tasha opened her mouth to speak but Tina stopped her, "Strange folks knocking on the door, all hours of the night, you two crying from either being hungry or scared of the dark... I finally started working under the table at that dank ass laundromat, cleaning up behind folks in the bathroom and outside, just to make sure y'all had somewhere to go after school."

Tina looked down at Tasha and rolled her eyes, "And here you is, crying about that little bit of change? I earned every bit of that money - looking after yo ass!"

The tremble in Trisha's voice was unmistakable, and Tasha knew she was on the verge of crying as she spoke. "What Kitty did messed us all up Tina, but what y'all did.."

"What WE did?!" Tina said incredulously. Leaning in toward Trisha, Tina's bitter laugh rippled throughout the tiny space between the three of them. "Is that how you wanna remember what happened?"

Trisha's eyes widened as she looked between Tina and Tasha. She said nothing as Tina went on. "After getting caught up on the bills and fixing what I could around the house, I had to fight Kitty for the rest of that change. So I treated myself and I don't regret nothing!"

Tasha gripped the sides of the table as she stood. Though before she left, something about what Tina said had to be addressed. Because the one thing Tasha could say she learned from Kitty's death was that tomorrow wasn't promised to any of them. And that alone was enough cause for her to lock eyes with Tina. If this was possibly the last time she would ever speak to her big sister, Tasha had to make sure Tina knew the whole story. No matter how much it was going to hurt them both in the process. Remembering the therapy session that she had with Doctor Richardson that unlocked the painful truth, Tasha blinked back the oncoming tears as she held Tina's glare.

"You think we don't remember what it was like then? How you looked after us?"

A stray tear escaped and Tasha brushed it away as she continued. "Do you even know why I chose to major in English in the first place?"

More tears fell as Tasha pushed her chair back while looking at Trisha and Tina.

"You two never read any of my scholarship essays, did you? They were all about my big and bright sister, 'Super T' and how she protected me from the big, bad world when I was too little to understand why it was so scary. How that led me to writing stories and my love of learning how to write better. So much so that all I wanted to do was to use my talents in storytelling with a pen to hopefully help others someday that found themselves lost in the darkness back to the light."

Feeling the heat of both of them staring up at her, Tasha pushed down the large lump in her throat. "You and Kitty taking the money ain't what hurts, Tina. It's the fact that as much as I wanted to leave town, if you had asked me then to give you the money, my dumb ass would have. All because of how much I worship you for taking care of me when Kitty couldn't."

The table was silent as her sisters processed what she had shared, and even though Tina's eyes no longer met her, Tasha knew she heard every word. Just as Tina was about to say something, Darnell and Devin rushed to the table.

"Mama, Titi! We need more money!"

Tina used that moment to step away from the railing, wiping her eyes.

"Not right now, y'all. Go sit inside for a minute." Trisha told them quickly.

When the boys started to walk over to the empty table, away from them, Tina laughed. Hearing the sound made Tasha's heart ache even more than it already did.

"Nah Trisha, go ahead and finish spoiling them with Tasha's cash. Ain't no telling how long she's gonna be here, gotta make sure to get all you can."

Not bothering to wipe away the hot angry tears that trailed down her cheeks, Tasha stared hard at Tina. *I tried. Lord knows I really tried this time.*

Standing up and reaching into her pocket, Tasha took out a few more bills and placed them on the table. "Enjoy lunch."

"Tash, please stay." Trisha pleaded.

Tasha ignored her as she turned to face their older sister instead. "Go to hell."

Trisha and Tina looked on as she picked up her helmet. Before turning to face Devin and Darnell, Tasha grabbed a napkin from the table and dabbed at her wet cheeks. Walking over to the boys, she gave each of them a kiss on the crown of their heads. "Titi's gotta go. See y'all again soon, okay?"

"Why you gotta go?" Devin asked softly.

Her heart ached seeing the confusion in his warm brown irises. Rarely was Tasha loss for words, but she was at that moment. *How do you tell a kid that you're all messed up because the person who was supposed to raise you failed?*

"I have to help Auntie Alexa and Rachel with something."

It wasn't a lie, but it wasn't the truth either. Tasha leaned down again and kissed Devin's forehead.

"Love you."

Sofie

Two weeks after hearing about Trap Sons album party from Regine, Sofie got out of bed when her alarm began going off, reminding her that she did have something to do that day. Now that they had potty trained Ro, she could enroll him in Pre-Kindergarten at Woods Edge Elementary.

She loved her little boy, but it was time for Sofie to get back to having her own life. And the sooner Sofie got Ro signed up for school, the sooner she could get back to getting the figure eight body she had before she was pregnant.

Quickly getting dressed and hopping into the SUV, Sofie drove Ro to her mama's house and dropped him off before heading to the school with all of his paperwork. As she was walking to the entrance, some idiot on a motorcycle came flying through the parking lot, causing her to drop a few of the documents.

Who rides a damn motorcycle to a kids' school anyway?

Rolling her eyes, Sofie bent down to pick up the paperwork. Once she did, she noticed the person hopping off of the bike and taking off their helmet. Curious, Sofie continued to stare at the woman as she reached into the backseat of the motorcycle and took out a medium-sized messenger bag. The woman placed the bag over her shoulder and put the helmet inside the seat, locking it with a key before turning to walk toward the building.

Sofie had never seen Tasha Daye in person, but she knew it was her. After hearing one too many of them uppity negroes at Christ Corner talk about Tasha inside the ladies' restroom during her first visit, Sofie looked her up online.

What's this bitch doing here?!

Soon Tasha walked past her, offering a small head nod, which Sofie didn't return. Instead of frowning as Sofie hoped she would, Tasha smiled at her, causing Sofie to deepen the crease on her forehead.

She waited until Tasha opened the main entrance door and followed behind her, listening in as she took her ID out of her bag and spoke to the front desk clerk, a short woman, with salt and pepper hair and a pair of reading glasses on the top of her head.

"Morning! My name's Tasha. Tasha Daye. I'm here for Mrs. Wallace's Professional Day. Here is my business card and my ID, as the school requested."

Sofie watched as Tasha smiled at the clerk.

"I'm not too late, am I?" Tasha asked.

The older woman placed the business card into a small envelope before handing back the ID. She was all smiles when she answered, "You right on time, baby girl. Mrs. Wallace's class is down this here hall. You'll see a sign for today's class, so just gone right in."

"Thank you." Tasha said, as she walked straight ahead.

She just takes pics of half naked hoes. Why would she be here for a 'Professional' anything?

Lost in thought, Sofie didn't hear the older woman call out to her until she did so for a second time.

"You lost girl?" The woman asked, raising her voice.

Hearing the woman call her 'girl' pulled Sofie out of her thoughts, as she whipped her head toward the older woman.

"Nah, I ain't lost. And I'm a grown ass woman, don't be calling me 'girl'!" she snapped.

The woman looked at her for a second before closing her eyes and sighing. "How may I help you, Miss?"

Sofie didn't miss the monotone voice the woman addressed her in, but she wanted to get this over with. Shoving the paperwork along with her ID at the woman, Sofie straightened her stance as she eyed the older woman. "I'm *Mrs.* Jerome Grant. Here to enroll my son into Pre-K as soon as possible."

Tasha

The sign for Professionals' Day was down the hall, as the woman at the front desk stated. Tasha took a peek inside the class before walking in. When Devin spotted her, Tasha's heart grew heavy from the sight of him jumping up and waving at her. Putting a finger in front of her lips, Tasha used her other hand to remind Devin to sit down.

While the adult in front of the class talked about what they did for a living, Tasha used that time to set up her equipment. Though as soon as she had her laptop up and turned on her portable projector, clapping could be heard around her before Mrs. Wallace spoke, "Thank you Mr. Aalegra for that wonderful lecture on working in architectural design! Up next, we have Devin's guest. Devin, please come to the front and introduce them."

Tasha watched as her nephew made his way to the front of the class and grinned as Devin spoke, "My titi -"

"Aunt." Mrs. Wallace corrected.

"My AUNT," Devin said loudly, causing the other children to laugh, "is here today. She takes pictures all over the world."

Tasha walked over to Devin, and she placed her laptop down on the empty desk and her messenger bag in the chair behind her. Balling her fist, Tasha reached down to Devin as he brought his tiny fist to connect with hers. "Thanks D."

When he returned to his seat, Tasha double checked her laptop and aimed the projector at the whiteboard, before smiling at the students. "My name is Tasha Daye. But those closest to me know me as Titi, or Titi Tasha."

The kids laughed again and the slide show that she created days ago began playing on the screen, causing a few quick whispers to fall over the group. "For four years, I've been lucky enough to work as an international photographer."

As more pictures showed up on the screen, Tasha briefly told them about when and where each photo was taken. The woman that Tasha saw earlier on her way to the class was also in attendance. She kept staring at her, but Tasha brushed it off as she went on, making sure to slowly explain to the kids the basics of being a photographer. When the slide show ended, Tasha asked the audience, "What questions do you all have?"

A little girl, almost half of Tasha's five feet nine frame, stood up before blurting out, "Are you married?"

Blinking several times, Tasha answered, "No, I'm not married."

"Why not?" A boy with cornrows asked.

"Well, I don't want to be married, I guess."

Tasha managed to squeak out before another boy with a pair of thick blue glasses suddenly spoke, "You can't really be a photographer. I ain't never seen a girl photographer before."

Tasha tried to keep her 'teacher face' on display as she looked directly at the young boy, "Firstly, anyone can be a photographer, and second, just because you've never met a woman photographer before doesn't mean that we don't exist."

Mrs. Wallace could be seen opening and closing her hand at Tasha, which she took to mean that she had five minutes left. Movement from her left hand side caught her attention, and as she looked over in that direction, Tasha saw the woman that was staring at her earlier quietly slip back out of the classroom.

"That is all the time we have for questions, but I do have a small gift for you all before I go. Devin, could you help me pass these out, please?"

Devin hopped out of his seat and sprinted toward Tasha, who handed him several small silver keychains. Each one was engraved with her matra *Inspiration is always a click away. Don't be afraid to capture it.*, as well as her initials.

When Mrs. Wallace stood, Tasha handed the last student their keychain before making her way back to the front of the class. "Thank you all so much for welcoming me into your classroom today."

Picking up her bag, Tasha quickly scooped up her projector and laptop as she went to sit in the back of the classroom to listen as someone else talked about what they did for a living. Once they wrapped up their presentation, a low bell rang throughout the building.

"Guest, please stand. That's the lunch bell, signaling the end of our time today. Thank you all for attending Professionals' Day and have a great day. Wave goodbye class." Mrs. Wallace said, turning to lead the children out of the room.

On her way out, Tasha stopped by the front desk and thanked the older woman for their help.

"Oh, I am happy to do it, baby."

As Tasha began to head out, the woman called out to her. Turning around to look at the older woman, she smiled. "I'm sorry. Do I need to sign out?"

"Oh, no, not that. The school is trying to raise money to get more netbooks for the kids with a fundraiser, and I wanted to ask if you would be willing to donate your time for the event."

As long as it's before the gala, it should be fine.

"I would love to help. What would you like me to do at this event, ma'am?"

The older woman brought her glasses down from the top of her head as she chuckled, "You can cut out all that "ma'am" business, for one thing. My name's Willie Mae."

"Yes, Ms. Willie Mae. How can I help?" Tasha asked again.

"Well, you say you a photographer, right?" Wilie Mae confirmed.

"Yes, ma- Ms. Willie Mae." Tasha corrected herself as Willie Mae chuckled again.

"Good, good. Then leave me another business card and I'll let the committee for the event know. They'll be in touch."

Tasha reached into her messenger bag and took out two business cards. Seeing that she still had a few extra keychains as well, Tasha grabbed one to give the older woman.

"I look forward to hearing from the event committee soon then."

Sofie

She spent the entire night side-eyeing her husband after seeing Tasha at Woods Edge elementary that morning. Every move he made, from giving her son a bath to the way he ate was under heavy scrutiny. He was usually easy to read, which helped Sofie when it came to getting more money for the month or knowing when to play nice where Evelyn was concerned. But if Jerome knew about his ex being back in time, he was doing a damn good job of hiding it. *He's acting like his regular degular boring self. So why am I wishing he was hiding something?*

Lost in her thoughts, Sofie didn't see Jerome as he made his way toward her on his way to his bedroom. "Is something wrong?"

Hearing his voice snapped her back to the present, and she quickly countered, "Why would you think something's wrong?"

"I can feel you watching me." Jerome bluntly replied before adding, "Do you need money again?"

Sofie narrowed her eyes as she jerked her head backward. "No, I don't need money." Not liking being on the defensive, she blurted out the first thing that came to mind, "Just trying to figure out when you gonna tell me about Buckem's album release party."

She watched as Jerome's shoulders dropped. *Maybe he really doesn't know about ole girl being back in town.*

"The invites just went out. And I ain't tell you because I'm not going."

He walked past her and opened the door along the opposite wall to his room, but Sofie wasn't done.

"Why? Regine says it's supposed to be a big event and that everyone from your label is going. It would be nice if you took me out for a change."

When he turned to look at her, Sofie felt like she was seeing him for the first time in years. He let out a heavy sigh and her eyes went to his chest. Soon she was checking out the rest of her husband's well toned frame. He may be lame, but Jerome was always easy on the eyes, even if he wasn't six feet tall or had a mouth full of grillz, like the dudes she was used to. *Looks like he's been hitting the gym hard lately.*

Her thoughts briefly turned to how she might be able to persuade Jerome into taking her to the album party. While she was remembering the few things he liked when they were sweating out her hair together, Jerome spoke. "Sofie, I'm not going. So what would it look like for you to be there without me?"

Before she could get out another word out, he walked into his bedroom and shut the door.

. . ◦﹏◦ . .

THE NEXT DAY, SOFIE got the call that her son's paperwork was verified and Ro could start Pre-K as early as that afternoon. She made sure to wake up early to get him ready for his first day of school. Her little man didn't seem to mind the change in their schedule, as he walked beside her into the colorful classroom. The Pre-K teachers introduced themselves to him, and just in case he got uncomfortable or scared, she stayed behind at a desk a few feet away while they included him in their normal class session. After almost an hour and not so much as a wail or backward glance to her, Sofie snuck out of the classroom to leave. She almost did the electric slide as she thought about how she would spend her weekdays now that Ro was officially in school.

Time to get my body right at the gym with my girl Regine! Thank you Jesus!

Though as she was walking down the hall to leave, the woman at the front desk called out to her. "Mrs. Grant?"

I see she learned to address me correctly.

Sofie grinned as she turned around slowly to answer. "Yeah. What else y'all need?"

The older woman sighed. "Well, the school is holding a fundraiser -"

"I ain't got no money."

She watched as the woman blinked several times before continuing, "You misunderstand. We are looking for volunteers to help us the day of the event. And I remembered that you were married to a local celebrity..."

Sofie rolled her eyes. "So you want my husband to write a check? Okay."

The older woman then pushed a flyer toward her. "Our scheduled entertainment had a last minute emergency, and I was hoping that your husband would be willing to join the lineup."

A bell then chimed throughout the building, and the classroom doors opened. Dozens of kids sprinted past her, screaming and crowding the hallway.

Ugh! Where all these damn kids came from?

Thinking quickly, Sofie took the flyer from the woman. "I'll tell him about it later."

Turning on her heel, she made a beeline to the exit before more kids came near her.

Faded Pictures

Tasha

A week later, Tasha found herself standing outside at the 'locally famous' Seafood Shack. She was twenty minutes early, but Tasha didn't mind. Using that time to process what she was feeling, like she had learned with her therapist, Tasha realized that when she first left home, it wasn't just Jerome she didn't say goodbye to, but to Evelyn too.

Seeing her again and having time to reconnect was a gift, one that Tasha would continue to be thankful for. And after her visit to Bottom's Up, Tasha had called Evelyn the following morning and shared as much as she could about Jerome's whereabouts like she promised she would. Once she was finished, Evelyn asked to see her, thanking her for keeping her promise. To know that she enjoyed spending time with her as much as she did warmed Tasha's heart. So, of course she had no problem making time to see the older woman as soon as possible.

After a few minutes, she saw Evelyn's car pull into the small parking area. Rushing to the driver's side of the car, Tasha opened the door and waited for Evelyn to get out. The older woman's laugh was light as she greeted Tasha, "Well, hello to you too!"

"Hey again Mrs. Evelyn." Tasha said with a smile.

The older woman glanced between Tasha and the motorcycle before shaking her head. "Baby, you ain't scared to ride around on that thing?"

Tasha laughed, "Not at all! I like living in the fast lane."

"You have to, I guess, to be riding around on that there bike." Evelyn narrowed her eyes down as she noticed Tasha's helmet. "At least you're being smart about it."

After the two stepped inside the restaurant, they were escorted to a table and seated.

"So, I want to hear about what you've been up to since you left - don't leave out nothing!" Evelyn finally said to Tasha.

Tasha told Mrs. Evelyn all about her travels, including her slowly learning Spanish and taking photos of all the places she dreamed of visiting back in high school.

She watched as Evelyn listened to her before the older woman asked, "Do you have any photos that I can look at?" Beaming, Tasha took her tablet from her bag and turned it on. "I always keep my portfolio ready - that's part of the job." She replied before entering her password.

Tasha handed Evelyn the tablet after she selected the General folder and let her browse through the pictures. Wordlessly, Evelyn stared at the pictures and Tasha worried that she may have clicked on the wrong folder. "Is everything alright Mrs. Evelyn?" She asked as gently as she could.

The woman put down the tablet and placed Tasha's hands into hers.

"I'm happy for you baby, that's all. I know leaving wasn't easy, but you had to follow your heart."

Tasha squeezed their hands together as she looked at Evelyn.

"Now that I've had time to look back, I shouldn't have been surprised when Eva left for New York," Evelyn said.

Curious, Tasha looked on patiently as Evelyn continued. "When she was little, I would show her pictures of the city all the time. Ever since I was in high school and learned that that's where all the great performers lived. But when I graduated from high school, my daddy introduced me to Jerome and that was that."

Tasha felt a wave of sadness wash over her as she saw Evelyn blink away tears.

"You did get to visit New York eventually, right? I remember-"

Thinking back to her time with Jerome wasn't the problem, it was having to talk about it with someone else. Especially his mama. Evelyn smiled sweetly at Tasha and answered her question.

"Yes, I finally did make it to New York to see my daughter and grandbaby. That was one of the best weeks of my life. But New York wasn't as I had pictured it."

Tasha had to ask, "How was it? Compared to what you thought it'd be like?"

Evelyn chuckled as she replied, "It was busy and alive with all sorts of folks, but none of that compared to meeting Marcus and my grandbaby."

Tasha's hands started to get sweaty, so she went to pull them away, only to have the older woman hold them tighter in to her own.

"I know you loved my boy, but I was hoping to call you my daughter someday."

Tasha's chest tightened as Evelyn continued, "Seeing you today, I wanted to be sure to tell you that. I'm happy that you went out and saw the world, I truly am, but I can't help but wish things had been different."

"Me too." Tasha whispered.

.. ⌘ ..

JEROME

Driving home to see his son after leaving the studio, Jerome took his time. With all the windows in his SUV open, he inhaled the crisp scent of clean air and enjoyed the little rays of sunshine that landed on his wrist as he waited at the red light. Driving past the plaza, Jerome thought he saw Evelyn's car parked outside The Seafood Shack.

Should I surprise her by coming in and paying for her and her friends' lunch?

Making a U-turn at the next light, Jerome pulled into the restaurant's parking lot and got out of his ride. Luckily, it was still early and not a lot of people were out, so he was able to step inside without being seen. Though once the doors closed behind him, Jerome wished there was a mob of fans waiting for him outside instead of the sight in front of him.

Seeing mama laugh as Tasha talked to her while they shared a seafood boil, Jerome went still. The two women were so caught up in whatever they were talking about that they didn't seem to notice anyone else around them. Jerome watched mama sign something to Tasha, who snorted, causing them to burst out laughing. He was too far away to hear what they were saying, but whatever Tasha said to mama next caused her face to soften. She then put more food on Tasha's plate, who beamed up at her.

She's still beautiful.

He didn't try to fight the memories of being with Tasha years ago as they rose to the front of his mind. The night they met, when she was working inside a food truck outside of Bottom's Up and threatened to call the law on him and several dudes from the bachelor party he'd attended. Jerome thought that was the last time he would be in her presence, but it was only the beginning.

Days later at Christ Corner, he found out that Senior, his daddy, had hired her to tutor the kids that went to their church. And after weeks of her standoffish behavior toward him, they became friends. To see her be so patient and passionate about tutoring her students, pouring encouragement in to them, and having that extend to him at a time when everything and everyone seemed to be working against him, it didn't take long for his feelings to deepen. The two of them soon danced on the line of friends and something more, before he finally had to tell her how he felt.

Those months of being with Tasha were bliss. Not just kissing and holding her as often as he could, but the way she loved him then. Jerome never met anyone as fiercely loyal and protective as Tasha. With everything that she had to face, from being judged by everyone in town for her mama's sins to even Senior firing her after the congregation demanded it to save face - she still loved him completely. The day she allowed herself to lean on him and let him in fully... It shocked him to the core and left Jerome pleading with her to spend forever with him. Thoughts of their last night together, at the bed and breakfast out on Bejon Beach made him shiver with a need he'd almost forgotten he could have for another.

A strong gust of wind blasted Jerome out of his thoughts as more people entered the restaurant, and he took that as his cue to exit.

Not making eye contact with the small group that walked in, Jerome quickly marched to his SUV. Once inside and seated, he took a few deep breaths before starting the engine and gripping the steering wheel. His lungs burned for a drink, but Jerome couldn't put off going home much longer. Sofie had sent him several messages, and he knew what she was like when left waiting for too long.

Besides, his little man would be there, and Jerome promised himself that he would not drink around Ro. *I can do this. For him, I will bear all of this.*

Waiting for the red light to change, Tasha's face flashed before him as the light changed. The drive home was short and made him miss his old place across town something fierce.

As he was stepping out of his kicks, Jerome heard Sofie stomp toward him from behind. He hadn't turned around to face her before she demanded, "What the hell took you so long?"

"Hey Sofie." Jerome replied as cheerfully as he could.

"You ain't gonna answer my question?"

"Met new producers at the studio."

Sighing deeply, Jerome followed the sounds of his son in the den. His namesake was happily playing with a few scattered coloring blocks. Not wanting to argue with Sofie, Jerome sat down next to Ro and joined him in trying to stack the blocks on top of each other. Just as he placed the last one on the already wobbly tower, they all came crashing down. Ro's amused giggles erupted throughout their home. His wife's laughter followed as she walked over to them and for a brief moment Jerome locked eyes with Sofie. *When did things get like this between us?*

The two had first met backstage at his first concert after signing with the label. He thought that she looked as sad as he felt. So Jerome sat next to her after performing and asked her what she thought about his performance. Her reply surprised him.

"Why? If you think it was good then what I think shouldn't matter."

Curious, Jerome nodded, "Yeah, but I want to know."

Sofie then looked up at him and laughed. "Your lyrics are different but the beats sound just like everyone else's here. I say change that before whoever you trying to reach stop trying to hear you."

He then asked for her number and the two started dating soon after. It wasn't long before folks saw them out on dates around town whenever he was in between tours. Months went by and Jerome eventually began attending church with her.

Their wedding was quick and held at Christ Corner, just as Sofie had asked. No one suspected what his mama had asked the two directly. Jerome could still remember seeing the proud smile on Senior's face as he pronounced them husband and wife.

Jerome Earl Grant the third, arrived while Jerome was at a worship festival, two months earlier than expected. When he got the news, he dropped everything and took the next flight home to be by his wife's side. Him and Sofie lived at the hospital as they prayed for Ro to become healthy enough to come home.

They were a team then, inseparable.

Though once Ro's first birthday came and went, things changed. The hospital bills still needed to be paid and Ro was spending more and more time at his mother-in-laws house than with Sofie. Things were being said about his wife that Jerome didn't want to hear, so he welcomed touring again.

They hadn't slept in the same room or so much as held hands in well over a year, but Jerome didn't care. *As long as my namesake is taken care of, I'll continue to provide.*

Thank You

• • ❧ • •

I HOPE YOU'VE ENJOYED reading *A Season to Love* and the excerpt to *Doves Cry Too*!

Please consider leaving the gift of an honest review of this read on your favorite website(s) this holiday season.

And I wish you many merry and bright days (and nights) of sweet reading!

Until next sigh,

K. McCoy

About The Author

. . ✿ . .

K. MCCOY IS A MULTI-genre author, who longs to live in a world where Black Womxn are celebrated and respected wholly. Through her indie author webinars, she helps other authors write drama filled, heart gripping, and authentic stories.

In her many years in self publishing, she has traveled around the world, crafting stories based on real-world experiences, combined with hopeful possibilities, while continuing to take part in several anthologies yearly. With goals to continue her travels and to see as much of the world as possible, K. McCoy hopes to continue writing amazing stories to share with their growing audience.

Learn more about K. McCoy at authorkmccoy.com.

Don't miss out!

Visit the website below and you can sign up to receive emails whenever K. McCoy publishes a new book. There's no charge and no obligation.

https://books2read.com/r/B-A-VWLI-NCBCC

BOOKS 2 READ

Connecting independent readers to independent writers.

Did you love *A Season to Love*? Then you should read *Holiday Bliss*[1] by K. McCoy et al.!

[2]

Discover four sensational indie authors in this Christmas Anthology!

Are you a reader that would love a little bit of merry and light, along with a dash of messy and spice?

Then go ahead and unwrap this holiday gift early!

Holiday Bliss features many well loved tropes - including enemies to lovers, secret crushes, family, and dark romance.

If those tropes ring your bells - go ahead and get comfy in your favorite snuggle attire, either solo or with your special someone as you explore how two reality TV show rivals learn that the real game between them is just beginning - days before Christmas. Along with a work mishap that brings two old crushes together, a daring rescue that

---

1. https://books2read.com/u/4N7yPG

2. https://books2read.com/u/4N7yPG

brings to light the dark truth for one married couple, and finds out what is waiting on the other side for another wedded pair once a snow storm ends on Christmas day.

These four fantastic reads have intriguing leading ladies and their own charming males, each promising a unique thrill with Christmas as a key element within the story. And along the way, every story will remind you why love is the true reason for the season.

No need to wait until Christmas Day - slip into your favorite sweater and cozy on up with *Holiday Bliss* today!

Also by K. McCoy

MAGIX
MAGIX
MAGIX: Melodic Whirlwinds

Standalone
A Dove's Cry
A Season to Love
Cupid's Kiss
Holiday Bliss
Doves Cry Too
The New E.R.A.

Watch for more at https://authorkmccoy.com.

Empowering dreams. Inspiring success.

About the Publisher

be a muse productions, LLC Established in 2024

A creative publishing company that looks to uplift independent authors and promote their stories to diverse readers.

Read more at https://beamuseproductions.wordpress.com/.